Photographs, cover & interior design by Cassandra Smith

Offset printed in the United States
by Edwards Brothers Malloy, Ann Arbor, Michigan
On 55# Enviro Natural 100% Recycled 100% PCW
Acid Free Archival Quality FSC Certified Paper

Published by Omnidawn Publishing, Richmond, California
www.omnidawn.com   (510) 237-5472   (800) 792-4957
10 9 8 7 6 5 4 3 2 1
ISBN: 978-1-890650-96-4

best american experimental writing

GUEST EDITED BY COLE SWENSEN
SERIES EDITORS: SETH ABRAMSON & JESSE DAMIANI

OMNIDAWN PUBLISHING
RICHMOND, CALIFORNIA
2014

Cole Swensen
Guest Editor's Introduction   11

Seth Abramson and Jesse Damiani
Series Editors' Introduction   16

~

Emily Abendroth
EXCLOSURE]22[21

CA Aiken
[hotspur]   23

Toby Altman
HABEAS CORPUS   24

Rae Armantrout
BETWEEN ISLANDS   26

Rebecca Bates
a pair of interacting   27

Charles Bernstein
Dea%r Fr~ien%d,   28
From **Duplexities**   29

Mei-mei Berssenbrugge
HELLO, THE ROSES   30

Nathan Blake
**"A Primers for What Now of This Instant By Which I
        Meaning Slaughter You Idiot"**   34

Amaranth Borsuk & Andy Fitch
May 16   38

John Bradley
Everything That Lists   40

Hannah Brooks-Motl
Twenty-Nine Sonnets of Etienne de la Boétie   41

Robert Bruno
WWW.MY/MY/MY.COM *Excerpt   42

C. S. Carrier
Soliloquies Delivered Simultaneously   46

Ken Chen
WE ENNUI   47

Maxine Chernoff
EVIDENCE   48

John Coletti
Ceravolo   49

CAConrad
isotherm pinpoints our mutual transudation   51

Kathryn Cowles
Glossary   52
Glossary   53

Mónica de la Torre
thewanderer   54

Brett DeFries
daimondead   55

LaTasha Diggs
damn right   it's betta than yours   56

Kate Durbin
from The Hills   57

Peter Eirich
[I see the light pink and green]   59

Lisa Fishman
[A scarecrow grew night by night in the field]   60

Ossian Foley
[threat upon horseback]   61
alef   62

Logan Fry
It Has a Face   63

Colin Fulton
Life Experience Coolant (condensed)   64

Forrest Gander
Raven   67

Angela Genusa
from Spam Bibliography   68

Lara Glenum
Guerilla This Guerilla That   70

Judith Goldman
Concilia   71

David Gorin
from DUST JACKETS   76

Kate Greenstreet
PLATE 1: STANDS AT HER HALF-DOOR   80

Brenda Hillman
Galaxies Are Born with Our Mother   83

Kevin Holden
from Orion Flux   84

Harmony Holliday
Niggas in Raincoats Reprise   85

Janis Butler Holm
Sound Poems   86

Darrel Alejandro Holnes
Middle Passage   87

Kathleen Janeschek
Your Life   91

Lisa Jarnot
The Oldest Door in Britain   94

Andrew Joron
THOUGHT THOU OUGHT   95

Douglas Kearney
EVERY HARD RAPPER'S FATHER EVER: FATHER
           OF THE YEAR   96

Daniel Khalastchi
Actual-Self Costume Party: 97

Paula Koneazny
nursery rune /   98

Jennifer Kronovet
Jean Berko Gleason 99

Ann Lauterbach
A Reading 100

Paul Legault
from What Dorothea Did 103

Shannon Maguire
philologist disaster 105

Farid Matuk
New Romantics 106

Kim Minkus
[we smash] *from* Laneway 107

Rajiv Mohabir
Homosexual Interracial Dating in the South in Two Voices
   (found poem) 110

Nicolas Mugavero
from Instructions for Killing your Wife 111

Laura Mullen
Sestina 114

Hoa Nguyen
TOWER SONNET 116

Jena Osman
Citizens United v. Federal Election Commission 117

Ron Padgett (translating Guillaume Apollinaire)
Inscription for the Tomb of the Painter Henri Rousseau
   Customs Inspector 120

Ed Pavlić
Words 46,740 thru 47,047—That's to Say Page 159—
   of a Novel-in-Progress 121

M. NourbeSe Philip
CROSSED STITCH 122

Vanessa Place
[No More] 124

Artur Punte
[When all night the wind fondles tin]
(translated by Matvei Yankelevich & Charles Bernstein) 125

Claudia Rankine
[You are in the dark]   126

Ed Roberson
Case   127

Elizabeth Robinson
Lynx rufus   129

Ryan Paul Schaefer
from County Habere   133

Danniel Schoonebeek
Thunderhead   136

Christopher Stackhouse
2:49pm   138

Chris Sylvester
from Still Life with Blog   139

Jennifer Tamayo
[JENNIFER TAMAYO, my love how are you]   143

Anne Waldman
from Gossamurmur   146

G.C. Waldrep
discrete series: CAPTAIN/DAHLIA   149

Marjorie Welish
Fray   150

[self-authored]
THE BECOMING   153

Lynn Xu
from NIGHT FALLS   155

Joey Yearous-Algozin
from Zero Dark 30 Pt. Font   157

~

ACKNOWLEDGMENTS   160

CONTRIBUTORS   164

Guest Editor's Introduction

The term "experiment" has a volatile history in American poetry—and, of course, it would be self-contradictory if it did not. The question, then, lurking behind a collection such as this is "what does the word 'experimental' mean now?" In 1841, Ralph Waldo Emerson cautioned his readers that " . . . I am only an experimenter. Do not set the least value on what I do . . ." and in the late 1880s, toward the end of his life, Walt Whitman declared to his good friend and biographer, Horace Traubel, "I sometimes think the Leaves is only a language experiment." Even Pound, with his often-cited injunction to "make it new," feared that his generation was "a generation of experimenters . . . unable to work out a code for action." As these comments illustrate, in the formational days of modern American literature—from the 19th through the early 20th centuries— the term "experiment" had a negative, even if occasionally jaunty, connotation. Preceded by qualifiers such as "only," it was regarded with a doubt that assumed its failure and deplored its uncertainty.

Fast-forward a hundred and fifty years: The presumptions of failure and uncertainty have not changed, but their values within their contemporary cultural milieu have. Failure and uncertainty in poetry are no longer seen as pejoratives; on the contrary, they are recognized as valuable modes of maintaining a text's openness, and are frequently the byproduct of a writer's attempt to resist predictability and complacency—two very real threats to vital artistic practice in our time. Such a dramatic shift in popular thinking highlights the cultural and social stability that we currently experience; from a fledgling culture for which stability quite simply equaled existence, the United States has developed one that, in little more than a century, has encouraged stability so vigorously that we've allowed it to stifle anything that doesn't resemble it, replicate it, and, ultimately and relentlessly, reinforce it. Except that such cultural and social stability is, of course, illusory; U.S. culture and society are more fragile now than they've ever been, and the guise of stability is fiercely produced precisely in order to mask that precariousness. Poetry that shies away from failure and uncertainty is often (and often unwittingly) contributing to language practices that hold that mask in place.

The concomitant result is that the term "experimental" has come full circle and is now heard by most as a term of high praise; it indicates work moving outward from fixed linguistic habits, on the cutting edge of poetic thinking. But that, in turn, is a notion that bears reexamination; the "cutting edge," you may say, is simply a metaphor; there is no violence intended—what is meant is the opening up of new directions, new fields of possibility—and yet no metaphor is simple, and given the historical specifics of North America, such a metaphor cannot but include another embedded one, that of "clearing new territory," with the long and unfortunate history of that tendency in the American psyche, which would have been readily recognizable to, for instance, Emerson and Whitman.

Implicit in this terminology is the concept of conquering, which is compounded by current usage, in which the term "experimental" is often paralleled by or conflated with the term "avant-garde," creating problematic associations with directly militaristic connections and implying that, whether you're in front or in the rear, the arts are all going in the same direction. These are aspects that this collection, in its implicit definition of contemporary experimentalism, questions and works to reconfigure.

And yet even if we acknowledge and work against the pervasive equations suggested above, the experimental can easily continue to fuel a feverish relationship to novelty, in which the different is seen to be, in itself, good: again, Pound's "make it new." (Though Pound did not "newly" make that phrase; he took it from the first emperor of the Shang dynasty circa 1750 BCE.) Works appearing over the past 15 years under the rubrics of "uncreative writing," "conceptual writing," and "flarf," as well as countless works that don't fit neatly under any classification, have modeled welcome exceptions to the blanket valorization of the new, and have helped refocus discussions of experimentalism around the question of what such writing is actually doing, a question that can easily become obfuscated by a fascination with difference for difference's sake.

The selections in this volume present contributions to the current world of progressive writing that are largely distanced from both the fixation on novelty and the metaphor of territorial expansion, and as such, they are helping to rewrite the experimental idiom, replacing earlier paradigms with others acknowledging, supporting, and extending a civic model that offers alternatives to that of the rugged individualist (still dominant in American popular culture) in favor of one that explores various modes of dispersed collectivity.

Though marvelously diverse in their ways of addressing, enabling, and actualizing such a collectivity, the poets presented here share certain common points, the most prominent among them being a focus on the reconfiguration of subjectivity. For many progressive writers in North America, the invitation to reconsider subjectivity came through mid- to late-20th-century European poststructuralist and postmodernist theoretical and philosophical writings, filtered into the ambient poetic conversation through university English and philosophy departments and, for many, through the work of the Language poets. The latters' complex interests included the materiality of language, the rights of the signifier, the problematics of referentiality, and a critique of the constructed nature of linguistic coherence and of the subjects who produce it. I go back through this history, no doubt known to most readers here, largely to address the size of "now." What do we mean by "contemporary"? In the past 100 years, in most areas of life, time has become increasingly compressed, exponentially so, but this is much less true in the arts at every level other than that of fashion. This is not to denigrate fashion—its proper point is speed and mutation, instability and ephemerality—but to make a distinction that highlights the artistic components of sustained and sustaining culture, in which the contemporary is a long, evolutionary glide. Change may begin with an apparently dramatic or radical shift, but it becomes substantive change only gradually, almost imperceptibly, though, usually, irreversibly.

Which means that the roots of the most vital works today, if they are rooted firmly, necessarily go back decades. In particular, while most of the issues of concern to the experimental writers of the 1980s listed above have been carried forward in one way or another by much subsequent experimental writing, none has been as widely treated as the question of the construction and meaning of the I. This is because it was not only a critical question for post-structuralism and postmodernism; it was also, and still is, a crucial question for American society. While reconsiderations of the role of the individual in America can be seen emerging in the literary revolutions of the Beat Poets, Black Mountain, the New York School, the San Francisco Renaissance, and the Black Arts Movement, much more important were the Civil Rights movement and the Women's Liberation movement in the 1960s and the Gay and Lesbian liberation movement of the 1970s—explosively divergent social revolutions with radically different needs for the most part, but one they shared was the need to redefine the possibilities for and the nature of the individual in relation to the larger civic body. The celebration of the fiftieth anniversary of the Civil Rights Act this year gives us the opportunity to mark the enormous changes that have occurred in the ensuing half-century, but also to note arenas in which change has been far too little and too slow, and often because of the persistent paradigm of aggressive individuality that continues to put the interests of the individual above those of the community. Though a largely commercial movement, giving rise to a social one, the digital revolution has also contributed to the de-centering of the subject through the avatars and anonymities that its technologies enable, and even more importantly, through the distributed networking models that it has developed. Taken together, these and other societal changes have opened up possibilities for distributed subjectivities and networked identities that, whether good or bad in themselves, may have finally created room for an altered concept of the American "I."

To refuse the inheritance of aggressive individualism and move toward more socially responsive and inclusive identities is a political gesture, and much contemporary American experimental poetry makes it, not in the form of the polemical address, but rather in the much subtler, but ultimately more persistent, reconstitution of the polis as a dispersed system, more analogous to the computer-based distributive network mentioned above—we are a single thoughtful system, and the poems in this volume suggest several maps of that system and several plans for carrying it forward. These maps and plans have nothing to do with not using the "I" per se; instead, they focus on its reconstruction and its redeployment, exploring ways that it can move outward, beyond the individual body to emanate from the body politic, understanding that phrase not as a metaphor, but as a reference to a real body that we all actively inhabit.

Some of the experimental modes presented in the following pages already have an extensive history, such as the practice of appropriating language, remixing and recontextualizing it, effectively disengaging it from its original author without attaching it to another one, or the practice of erasure poetry, in which surface erosion reveals fragments of language in new perspectives and relationships, or the use of constantly shifting subject matter, creating a montage that approaches omniscience as it thwarts the accrual of a dominating authority. Other modes, such as documentary poetry, which in its outward focus functions at times as witness and often as a call to action, and research-based work, which gives voice to an archive, a history, a location, or other particulars, also speak from variable and ambiguous subject positions. Other equally powerful distributive strategies are often not recognized or discussed as such, for instance, translation, with its constant slippage creating a radically recontextualized hybrid voice, and ekphrasis, which decenters poetry in a stretch toward other media, raising questions about the boundaries of any given artistic practice. Other modes of complicating the self are harder to label; one writer here, through the obsessive repetition of the name of another, creates a wizard-of-Oz world in which everyone is Dorothea, while another obsessively uses her own name to create a critical distance that makes apparent the density of seemingly trivial social interactions. The I, too, figures among these poems, but suddenly it has no face; it has no personal history; instead, it constitutes a site of potential experience, with experience itself recognized as a flow passing through populations and situations in which an I is a function that organizes events, anchors perceptions, and balances other phenomena to create a dynamic moment of contingent elements.

There's anxiety inherent here too, for what much experimental work today proposes is an exteriorization of identity, which is not a matter of extending a personal identity to include that of others; it is to take seriously Gilles Deleuze's claim that "Life is not a personal thing." While the beauty of that line is immediately apparent, it is perhaps less easy to live. To cast the self outward—in the hope of encountering others in ways that un-other them—is a form of self-exile, which in itself engenders anxiety, but it's also a stance that mirrors ambient anxieties arising from numerous social pressures in play. When performed in poetry, because language is incapable of being just a mirror and is instead always augmentative, an aesthetic dimension is added to this state of self-exile. This is not to say that it is made attractive in any way, but that its internal constitutive relationships are highlighted over and above the elements related. In the process, anxiety is put back into motion (anxiety being, among other things, the stymied sensation resulting from excesses that can't be put to use), releasing its force and making it once again available.

Most of the poems in this volume emphasize language as a social practice, as something we do together. This shows up at times through the replay of public language, including stock phrases, familiar nursery rhymes, or inherited forms, and at other times through an inventive disruption of linguistic surface. Often this disruption is subtle, accomplished through slight non-sequitur, oblique connection, or slips of logic, and sometimes it's more dramatic, achieved through various kinds of syntactic rupture and semantic breakdown. By highlighting language as a circuit of exchange, such works replace the invisibility of "normal" language and the illusion of "natural" language with a recognition of its always-constructed state, implicitly asking us to question the who and why behind the language parading all around us as a natural normality. In short, such work functions as a call to action: it calls us to recognize language as part of the commons, like air or water; it is part of the whole body of shared resources that must never be privatized, and calls us to be vigilant against such privatization and to put constant effort into maintaining its health and functionality. As with our water and air, we must guard against its stagnation, for like water and air, it is a circulatory system essential to the vitality of the social body.

In addressing the question of the experimental, in provisionally groping toward a definition, I find myself constantly going back to the question of what poetry does, both as Wittgenstein might have meant it and as J.L. Austin might have meant it, because to ask what poetry does is to ask what language does, for poetry is the overt performance of language that makes all other language uses recognizable as performances as well. And yet only by performing language as itself (isolated from its utility) can we see that language is in fact performing us, and is therefore the site of the construction of that "us." The works here show us a larger, more flexible "us" that is, itself, part of the commons. To rewrite the Pound quotation above: This is a generation of experimenters, and this is its code for action.

Cole Swensen,
Guest Editor

Series Editors' Introduction

It's common practice for the Series Editors of "Best American" anthologies to emphasize that "best" and "American" indicate only that a work has been favored by a discrete class of persons, from a non-exhaustive pool of possibilities, at the close of a given calendar year. As the Series Co-Editors of this first edition of *Best American Experimental Writing*, we begin our consideration of the purpose and utility of such an anthology with the same caveat. In fact, we'd like to take things a bit further and concede that even the words "experimental" and "writing" implicitly demand that substantial pressure be placed upon them. What, after all, is "experimental" literature? Well, to offer readers of this volume a spoiler: neither this edition of *Best American Experimental Writing* nor future editions will attempt a comprehensive response to that important question, nor do we find possible answers to the question nearly as interesting as the question itself. While we're confident about several elements of the experimental ethos in creative writing— for instance, that it's a moving target; that it requires some form of risk be taken; that it quite often engages questions of form—we're most insistent on this one: that experimental writing is not circumscribed by a canon of authors, movements, poetics, or concepts. We approach experimental writing, instead, as a practice that renews itself perpetually in every culture with a literature.

Our hope, with this and future editions of *Best American Experimental Writing*, is to showcase individual works rather than focusing on individual personalities. If in fact artistic experimentation is a cultural phenomenon, rather than a quality of genius resident in only a select few, it makes more sense to speak of the breadth and depth of those subcultures in which such experimentation occurs, rather than of a canon of names to know or a series of compositional gestures that can or cannot reliably be termed "experimental." In broader terms, our feeling is that the best anthologies are open-ended adventures rather than codified admonitions, and so it's with this spirit of wonder and humility that we embark upon what we expect will be a years-long journey of discovery and delight.

Like most editors, we'd like to think that our work has a pedagogical function as well as a literary one. We believe that authors of all ages and stages of artistic development can benefit from an anthology that celebrates the exploratory authorial ethos without overdetermining or indeed even acknowledging its boundaries. We hope this anthology will do yeoman's work in starting conversations whose trajectories and endpoints are ineluctably uncertain. While every writer for whom the discussion of risk is a regular activity can and should have their own favorite poetry and prose to cite in such conversations—or, increasingly, cross-generic works broadly informed by an experimental ethos and praxis—merely reciting these favorite texts and their authors, rather than considering a generous cross-section of experimental writing, risks positioning literary experimentation as a formula rather than an investigation. So the challenge we take on here as editors is also the challenge we issue to our readers: to expand our capacity for surprise and our sense of the possible, rather than searching these pages for only those experiments that validate our own instincts or celebrate those authors we already consider our literary kin. We believe the best anthologies please few in this latter way, even as they lay down a gauntlet challenging us to be ever more audacious in our writing, reading, and synthesis.

We know that those committed to innovative writing face challenges less adventuresome authors do not. The financial and human resources available for the promotion of literature are still too scarce, and that's especially true for literature that's likely to frustrate reader expectations and find ardent supporters only among a scattered few. Publishers of innovative writing spend untold hours, energy, and hard-won monies to reach audiences that sometimes number only in the hundreds. As writers ourselves, we take on the task of editing this anthology mindful of how precious literary risk is—wherever it appears, and whatever its permutation—and that our endeavor can do no more than non-exhaustively honor a few such appearances and permutations. We hope to help publishers and authors of innovative writing advance the conversations they're already having in their own subcommunities, not to dictate who should be included in or excluded from these conversations. As to that, the answer is clear enough: conversation about the countless ways we can, do, and must push language should always remain open and inviting to all. We therefore anticipate, over the next few years, expanding the conversation this anthology series constitutes to the bursting point; this year's edition is just a first step, albeit an important one, in contributing to a dialogue that's been going on in North America and beyond for well over a century.

Our selection process for this anthology is, in keeping with the overarching mission of the project, a novel one. While 45 of the 75 poems appearing in each edition of *Best American Experimental Writing* are selected by the edition's Guest Editor, and 15 by the Series Co-Editors, another 15 are culled from a large pool of unsolicited and entirely "blind" submissions. It's important to us that any literary artist currently innovating feel she has access to this anthology, whether or not she participates in a literary community or, already playing a role in one, considers herself well-placed among its byzantine hierarchies. In reading the more than a thousand unsolicited submissions sent to the series this year—all of which were, like every work in *Best American Experimental Writing*, either unpublished or first published in the year preceding the anthology's release—we were consistently impressed with their quality. We wish that anyone worried about the longevity of the experimental spirit in literature could have read over our shoulders as we marveled at the extraordinary range of ambitions in the work we encountered. One reason we took the step of accepting blind submissions is that we know how many courageous authors never, despite all their courage, see their work read voraciously and with deliberation by editors of anthologies, nor even—in many cases—by editors of presses or literary magazines. This owes not to any fault on the part of anthologies, presses, or magazines, but merely the fact that North America is home to such a cacophony of literatures that it's easy for superlative work by relatively unknown or reticent authors to get lost in the mix. Our hope is to honor the efforts of the writers in this anthology by finding for them as wide an audience as we can, and then returning each year to do the same for another slate of what we consider exemplary works. We expect the result to be a diverse and exciting cross-section of authors, many of whom will be unfamiliar to even the most avid reader of experimental writing. We believe that's all to the good, not just because it creates new connections between individual writers and readers, but because it emphasizes the scope of the experiments now being authored in North America.

·

This anthology appears at a time of incomparable excitement in North American letters. Innovative writing today partakes not only of compositional methods but also methods of distribution that were unthinkable just three decades ago. Experimental writing is at its core reactive—dependent upon the existence of precedents in order to interrogate, critique, and undermine them—and the Information Age makes a generous understanding of literary precedent possible for a larger number of authors than ever before. The result is that even postmodernism, once thought of as an arcane literary theory accessible only to those in the ivory towers of academia, has long since passed the point of cultural crystallization. In many ways postmodernism, like its predecessor modernism, has been subsumed into the mainstream, even as we still see a plethora of discrete postmodernisms and modernisms in the innovative writing of today. We also see, however, many authors with an exploratory ethos striving to blend these inherited cultural paradigms into new modes of expression and meaning-making. The Internet has reshaped the literary landscape by expanding exponentially its capacity to record, generate, and juxtapose contexts. Artists can learn virtually from others in distant reaches of the globe, making fusion and appropriation critical hallmarks of our moment. The ensuing surfeit of content at times begets an interest in niche and genre over universality, at times a defiance of all three of these limits.

This confluence of opposites is indicative of our current cultural paradigm, one that seems to be notably different—which is not to say qualitatively better or worse— than what preceded it. Conventional binaries like sincerity and irony, optimism and cynicism, knowledge and doubt, sophistication and wildness, progress and tradition, and even Life and Art are being frustrated or superseded in a way that's exhilarating rather than enervating. Our relationship to data has shifted from a passive to an active one, as perpetual engagement with our many subcontexts (or a disengagement that carries with it the same apparent swirl of activity) introduces a novel texture to our negotiation of the public and private spheres. Our personal and communal histories are now recorded and therefore permanent—a culture of surveillance highlighted by Edward Snowden's recent leaks of classified NSA documents—and so the question is ever on the table, how do we react? And how do our reactions, whether in Life or Art or some format that inextricably conjoins the two, alter our understanding of both personal and political commitment? How do we find coherence, if at all, at a time when our selves are endlessly stratified and manipulated across increasingly disparate and specialized forms of social media?

With an eye toward these critical questions, we proceed, as editors, mindful of what the late David Foster Wallace predicted more than two decades ago:

> The next real literary 'rebels' in this country might well emerge as some weird bunch of anti-rebels, born oglers who dare somehow to back away from ironic watching, who have the childish gall actually to endorse and instantiate single-entendre principles.... Real rebels, as far as I can see, risk disapproval. The old postmodern insurgents risked the gasp and squeal: shock, disgust, outrage, censorship, accusations of socialism, anarchism, nihilism. Today's risks are different. The new rebels might be artists willing to risk the yawn, the rolled eyes, the cool smile, the nudged ribs...

In many of the works that appear in *Best American Experimental Writing 2014*, Internet detritus—whether it be the transmission-corrupted text of Charles Bernstein's "Dea%r Fr~ien%d"; the misspellings and apparent mistranslations of Nathan Blake's "A Primers for What Now of This Instant By Which I Meanting Slaughter You Idiot"; Robert Bruno's "matrix" barcodes, readable only by machines; or Chris Sylvester's non-interpretive hash of online and pop-culture ephemera—plays a crucial role in creating an oscillatory state between irony and sincerity, cynicism and optimism, artifice and authentic commitment. One neither believes nor mistrusts such detritus because, while deliberately and creatively sculpted, it is not, finally, voice-driven. By constantly gesturing at opposite poles, such texts situate themselves so ambiguously in the middle that we begin to question the utility of these poles in the first instance. This interest in mediation through oscillation transcends existing models for literary expression; indeed, new technologies have made it significantly easier for technophobes or ostensible "non-writers" to author creative works that deviate in compelling ways from conventional form. These deviations take diverse shapes in the anthology that follows: in addition to those works mentioned above, we find textual "noise" directed along highly delineated vectors (in Douglas Kearney's harrowing "Every Hard Rapper's Father Ever"); consequential alterations of our relationship with the page as a field for composition (in Joey Yearous-Algozin's *Zero Dark 30 Pt. Font*); and texts that juxtapose forms, concepts, and genres using a breed of literary tampering that's as inexplicably apt as it is mesmerizing (as in Angela Genusa's *Spam Bibliography*). These experiments speak, in their own ways, to the "metamodern" zeitgeist of our present cultural milieu.

Now more than ever, epistemological questions of "truth" and "meaning" lie in the hands of readers. Ultimately, intention matters less than a sublime ambiguity of affect; the fact that we question what is reasonable to believe of the literature we read invites rather than inhibits our attention to and engagement with the text, a state of affairs that might have been unthinkable to the average reader just fifteen years ago. The Internet has democratized not just metaphysical but affective spaces; if gone are the days when geography and financial resources alone dictated the availability of information, gone too is the hegemony of interlocutors, whether they be scholars, credentialed artists, or even canon-minded editors. In 2014, the chief currencies in literature are attention, awareness, and oscillation between forms, concepts, and genres that are as readily navigable and interchangeable as adjacent tabs on a web browser.

·

If there's one thing we hope is clear from all of the foregoing, it's that this anthology is not intended as a conclusive compendium of last year's innovative writing. No anthology could possibly hope to achieve that sort of comprehensiveness— nor would the project of celebrating innovation in literature be well-served by a philosophy that imagines comprehensiveness as desirable. There is, of course, no discrete rubric imaginable that could aid us in determining which works in a given span are the "best," as "best" is differentially defined depending upon the context of the utterance, and in any case rightly evolves over years and decades. We make no claims, then, for the work included in this anthology, other than this important one: that to be found here is a superlative if incomplete sampling of the types of formal and conceptual innovation now evident in contemporary North American writing. As a sampling rather than a canon, the emphasis in these pages is ever on the concepts and perspectives and provocative compositional phenomena of the works themselves, not the biographies or affiliations of their authors. No claim can or should be made about whether any of these pieces of writing will be broadly admired or even considered "experimental" many years hence, as far more important than the vagaries of posterity is the vibrancy of dialogues about literature in the present—and the vitality and reach of the subcommunities in which risk-prone literature is authored. No one can know how the future will speak of the present; what we can do today is simply generously document some of the most distinct and courageous experiments now being conducted by English-language writers, and hope that this documentation provides a critical tool— certainly in the present, and hopefully well into the future—to any writer seeking to pass along an experimental ethos to those with whom they live, work, and write.

Seth Abramson and Jesse Damiani,
Series Editors

Emily Abendroth

EXCLOSURE]22[

For a great many well-positioned and amply-propertied people on the planet,
       their own personal sense of risk tended to rise in near perfect
       inverse proportion to the actual threats that were posed around
       them. In other words, it was primarily those persons who had
       only rarely or never been the subject of physical trespass and
       attack that nevertheless tended to fear it all the more vehemently.
       Constantly proving themselves far and away the most willing
       to support the harshest injunctions or carceral punishments in the
       name of maintaining their own broadly jones'd for lack of exposure.

Whereas others, having been exposed, and in some cases, ceaselessly exposed,
       to nearly every form of available violence, were thus compelled
       by this experience to acknowledge that any notion of "individual"
       protection from violation, as divorced from a concept of collective
       health, was not only impossible, but a straight-up debacle. And
       further still, that the costs of attempting to build such personal
       fortresses of reprieve merely succeeded in enacting on other bodies
       another form of destructive aggression that was itself rarely named
       but whose painful range of maiming pressures were all too acutely
       felt,
              were welt-inducing even.

       Like a permanent belt caught up in the act of melting between
              gestures of constriction and beating.

These hardly fleeting distortions, both tedious and bleeding in nature
 were the somewhat unavoidable outcome of determinant dictums which reinforced
 the security of one door via the silent permission to viciously bash in another.

A motherlode of crudely isolated calculations

A defensive geometrics made thickly dense via the tricks of untraceable decimals
via their fraught wrestling onto paper in inexcusably tapered or abstract forms.

 And yet warm and worming beneath this surface of soft fluorescents
 bent in at the very edges of its tightly ledgered sentences and columns
 stood a populated scene of complex and teeming sentient bodies

scented bodies oscillating bodies erasing bodies migrating bodies embracing bodies

  each boring in turn new holes in the old numbers
  mumbling, by way of dissent:

  "In the event that the place of abode is the body itself
  how do we migrate?

  how do we swarm?"

CA Aiken

why I speak not good just many why my chest burns takes me
to the fire to the sparks between blows to riding at the edges
of dark why I fear my feet the fields the ground must stay atop
must clench and spur hold the rear buck forward for these
are words and as they blow out spew them as ember as tinder
they may catch ignite and they are lost to me letters so easy to
lose not a real fear as disgrace shame and turn them and form
them to lose them here it is warrior here hero here a man and
his horse a man and his sword fear and remembering that and
what else and nothing to lose here so run, mount, nothing left
to turn back to and this we call courage this we call bravery
this we call honor this we call trust this we call duty this we call
loyalty this we call glory

only how empty my palm when the weight held in lines falls
from me, how cold and free
only how hard the earth in the tangle of arms that makes loss
the stumble and embrace of fall

for defeat and loss become beyond what can be put to words—
and how useless— at end we will all fall all the rest fled no men
mother father lover hands empty a burden to the earth words
unable to call any of it back tongue straining to dirt and still
call all of us strong.

Toby Altman

HABEAS CORPUS

scene: the chorus gathers before St. Mary of the Lake, the morning of the funeral.

• *the chorus tests the savors of death*

chorus: Sweet Lizzy Lazarus three days dead,
smokin' a cigar and jumpin' on the bed;
    Lizzy on her horse with a hole in her head,
plug it with yr finger or suck out the bread.
        Sweet Lazarus, *veni foras*
      and show your mega-muscles to the crowd!
      Apples to apples, dust to dust:
    and Lazarus erupts from the golden cloud.
Will you stay, sweet Laz, and wash our cars?
Or take a cookie from the cookie jar?
Adam dared—Adam sat a spell upon the stairs,
and cursed, and cried, "Hey Liz, are you still there?"
   "L.'s gone out for cigarettes and coffee!"
   "Can't be," says A. "Oh yeah?" says Eve, "It be."

(that you might have the body)

• notes:

> In this monody, the learned author bewails the death of his
> friend, once drowned, unfortunately resurrected, and foretells
> his final assumption when, as he blanches his hoo-ha in the
> bath, he will be drawn into the heavens, affording us one
> last look at his ass. We have him—at the zenith of his power,
> *'flames in the forehead of the morning sky'*—here in the studio
> with us; he has asked to address the viewers at home.

> [*enter Lazarus in sweats and a Bulls jersey, still swaying from
> last night's libations*]: Somewhere something mundane
> is happening, violently and insistently. (I will not say
> where). Somewhere sweet gum paves the alleys of our
> antique bodies. Someone there (I will not say who) calls in
> a dreadful voice: '*Lazare, veni foras* and show your mega-
> muscles to the crowd. I will tell you a beautiful thing,
> Lazarus; then I will apologize; then I will tell you a story.
> Your body is an ellipsis, my body is an ellipsis: melancholy
> speaks itself.'

Rae Armantrout

BETWEEN ISLANDS

1

If every eighth element
listed by atomic weight

is noxious

is that proof of
intelligent design?

2

Here's your far-fetched plan,
glinting
in slanted light –

except "plan" is wrong.

Thought comes before
or after,

but you interpose
yourself

and that red hourglass
which you think nothing of.

3

Next to the thoroughfare,

between the shopping plaza
and the medical complex,

a man in a straw hat
leans
on a pink
pasteboard sign

with one
woman's shoe on it

and the word "Repair"

Rebecca Bates

a pair of interacting

galaxies.
rebecca bates exits the train at astoria-ditmars blvd. pushes a man on the
stairs—pushes a man coming up—pushes a man approaching pulling against
and the stair. it is a kind of murder triumph—gravity's ultimate. rebecca bates
is an elongated—

—a thin dust occurring. the man is a hot region shearing up a stair rebecca
bates shearing from the outer edges of a stair rebecca bates a hot tidal pushing
shapes sheared. two bodies. the outer edges of two bodies sheared two dust
tails streaming two bodies viewed side-on. rebecca bates and the man side-on
crashing—burst—thin elongated streaming dust on a stair—

—an image consists of gravity bodies side-on and matter sheared and matter
flung in opposites rebecca bates and the man. the matter flung out—the hot
regions have begun to crash together—the remnants.

Charles Bernstein

Dea%r Fr~ien%d,

I sa%w yo%r pixture on
wehb si;t; no.t su%re
whhc one & w~ant to
tal^k or mee.t ver~y so.on
I am old ma%n 57 year$
ba%d tooth & sme.ll
ma.ke vr,y hr.d t mee%t
people. I a,m wr$iter
wr$ite po%re%y an,d
email writ.in,g al>so
se{ll goo;d stocks v;;ry
che~p & prozac~ s%ince
I a$lso can^'t slee.p. bihg
bizness opportunity to
tel^l on~ly my fre;ndhs
if yo;u hav. som,e m@oney
to hehlp me/i expec%
prostr%ate c%ncer an;y da;y
nee~d mon~ey al.so m.y
broth.er in tr^.rble
willl snd y$ou my pi%cture
n.eed check f~irst
a.m poet wh;o l.ikes
yo.u al%%read#y
emmail m$e at swifftpllay
@ssorrow.tv
a.m nhow you.r freind
& soul mat.e --

Binggo

From Duplexities

I'm no more here
Than you are went
You no more there
Than when I'd gone
And yet we meet
In cross-crissed lines
Across these empty
Icons of time.

•

If anything I have done
Cancels what I feel
Then put me on a boat
Without a keel
And I will row my way back to you
Whatever else I do
Whatever else I do

Mei-mei Berssenbrugge

HELLO, THE ROSES

1

My soul radially whorls out to the edges of my body, according to the same laws by which stars shine, communicating with my body by emanation.

When you see her, you feel the impact of what visual can mean.

Invisibility comes through of deep pink or a color I see clairvoyantly.

This felt sense at seeing the rose extends, because light in the DNA of my cells receives light frequencies of the flower as a hologram.

The entire rose, petals in moving air, emotion of perfume records as a sphere, so when I recall the emotion, I touch dimensionality.

From a small bud emerges a tight wound bundle of babyskin coral petals, held in a half globe, as if by cupped hands.

Then petals are innumerable, loose, double, sumptuous, unified.

I look through parted fingers to soften my gaze, so slow light shining off the object is filtered; then with feeling I look at swift color there.

It's swiftness that seems still as noon light, because my seeing travels at the same speed.

I make a reciprocal balance between light falling on the back of my eye to optic nerve to pineal gland, radiance stepping down to matter, and my future self opening out from this sight.

A moment extends to time passing as sense impression of a rose, including new joys where imagined roses, roses I haven't yet seen or seen in books record as my experience.

Then experience is revelation, because plants and people have in their cells particles of light that can become coherent, that radiate out physically and also with the creativity of metaphor, as in a beam of light holographically, i.e. by intuition, in which I inhale the perfume of the Bourbon rose, then try to separate what is scent, sense, and what you call memory, what is emotion, where in a dialogue like touching is it so vibratory and so absorbent of my attention and longing, with impressions like fingerprints all over.

I'm saying physical perception is the data of my embodiment, whereas for the rose, scarlet itself is matter.

2

The rose communicates instantly with the woman by sight, collapsing its boundaries, and the woman widens her boundaries.

Her "rate of perception" slows down, because of its complexity.

There's a feeling of touching and being touched, the shadings of color she can sense from touch.

There's an affinity between awareness and blossom.

The rose symbolizes the light of this self-affinity.

I come to visit drooping white cabbage roses at dusk.

That corner of the garden glows with a quality of light I might see when light shines through mist or in early morning reflects off water.

I stand quietly and allow this quality to permeate air around me.

Here, with a white rose, color is clairsentient, this color in the process of being expressed, like seeing Venus in the day.

Walking, I move in and out of negative space around which each rose is engaged and become uncertain of my physical extent as an object.

Look at the energy between people and plants; your heart moves into depth perception; for depth, read speed of light.

I set my intention through this sense of moving into coherence with the bio-photons of a plant and generate feeling in response.

A space opens and awareness gathers it in, as at night my dream is colorless and weaves into the nuance.

I can intentionally engage with the coherence of light beams, instant as though lightless, or the colored light of a dimension not yet arrived, as our hearts are not outside affinity with respect to wavelength, shaping meaning, using the capacity for feeling to sense its potency in a rose and to cultivate inter-being with summer perfume.

Nathan Blake

"A Primers for What Now of This Instant By Which I Meanting Slaughter You Idiot"

Okay wells I didn't knew if you has witness or not but there are like slaughter transpired right now outsides your window and I'm talk way nastier individual without heads throat and asses clutters the lawn where you wouldn't daily seen them sort of a things yet really I guesses it have already transpiring as you yourself are dead and rot and is just like spirit or whatevering's left up inside you meat after you've clock out for exampled me so I'll sorry to being the poor news borer of this instant but there you give it your been dead forever and evered chiefs and I'm like really truly sorrow.

Why even though should I been the individual who of this instant are like really truly sorrow when it's you who is total begged for thin ice and purchaser every alive individual like a whole fifty ton of it saysing craps liked No Peace Without Freedoms and Don't Treaded On Me and et cetera right into these faceshield of uniforms individual clutch their automatical weapon plussed boots shine all overt with bloodmucks prepare to kick some seriously asses and says all those craps even before then?

Like you idiot.

Neverminds took a look rightly outside your very own window if you weren't believe what it's I am talked about while I floats or sort of like vibrating in this cornered which are dues to my intensingly angers display at also to been dead forever myself because of all them writtened checks with your mouths your ass could not cashing BOOM I AM BLOWED UP THAT LAMP BESIDE YOURSELF WITH MINE MIND FOCUSES CAN YOU FELT IT!

And by a way thank a bunches for that for really okay lets me told you.

For you and likes much million other individual quoten upon television and radio during what you refers to protest solidarities civical dutied etc. and when them was took from us the internets and magazine next which was toughed because of importantly stuffs likes football kickass shoes bikini and etc. and when them were forbid too what about that littling slip of paper pass hands to hands or even just use with your mouth to yelling things with innocent which guesses what no one even really gived a care for when alive and now we is just clock out and still none one gived a care and that's what's I for one are like thankful for dues to me being total interest in what you has to sayed NOT!

BOOM THERE IS GOING ANOTHER LAMPS!

Listens I will gived these words correct as they are caming out of my mouth because it to be important for you heard them you idiot even though I founds difficult for me to gived out these words correct as because the statics shined all the time inside my skull now that I stooded clock out here alongsides you when it feel like an individual are digging a fishhooks through yours brain like on a treasured hunter except like there ain't any treasured to find oh well kept on digging I'll guess fine by me.

Whose are I kidding you yourself had already feelings it for sure I bet or just waited a little longer you will.

There will probable many thing you wonder of this instant and I is deliver here rightly in your very owned homes for counselor dues to you've clock out tonight of some idiot thinged you do and I am clock out many many day now and becomes super at it so kept up you idiot in case my geniused destroy you feeble heads which like who can blaming you BOOM BEWARES DID YOUR SAW THAT WARNING FROM ME?

Sometime I myself could saw from mine apartment window where a birdhouses using to stood with it little birds so happiness and pride like plops out egg hered and thered lalalalala ruffling them feathers and etc. and see instead in that places fire spin on a individual's heads stucked there unto the post because some other individual with opinion did thus to pronouncing somethings like I AM THIS UPSET!

If that were you then your like suck your freaker idiot and if its weren't you well then okay your are stills just a plained idiot.

As if it's even mattered for me right now sees as how you and me shared the similar boat which are that we aren't even gone on alive like expecting whenever you awoken each day think for granted well it sure are splendid to be a alive individual this very moments look at that sun right there pulsed so shinier and kickass and that homeless idiots want for pockets change even though stop whined it's a really great sidewalked he's be homeless on and those chipmunk humpings one anothers so feverely like they explode if they doesn't get all their humpings out this instant and I am missed witnessing those so much!

What I myself for one would gave to see some chipmunk humpings right of this instant not like a sick things but to proving that sure I've a alive individual.

Well I guesses like toughed titties for me whose never gave a care about any politicaled mess other than wanting to seen televisioning at night or player pokers by mine bud Tim and mine bud Rob except that have to stopped when them tracers began explode atop my apartments building ever ten minute to scary out them idiots and uniforms individual breaken downed our doors with automatical weapon up in my faces and sayed Remove You Yourselfs From This Premises Or Else then takes away all the foods oils weapon children and etc. upon the premises overed and overed and mine bud Tim and mine bud Rob were like we've done with those mess seen all many good buds been hitted and killed by uniforms individual so both want ahead and not removed them themselves from this premises when told by swallowing them like fifty bullet eaches because of how poor to been a alive individual and there were nothing for me to do of that instant alone but just sat atop a trashcans and count how long is there quiet in between bangs bangs bang.

Until I too have clock out I am not sure howed but duh here's I am.

BOOM I AM BROKE THE HELL FROM THEM LAMP OF THIS INSTANT WATCHING AND LEARNS FROM MY SUPER TECHNIQUED!

You wanting to be expert at these clock out and knew what to does with your yourself of this instant well firstly of all just forgot all them names place buds bikini and etc. from before becaused like they are sayonara to you yourself now for instant if you wants to thought about a boyfriend or girlfriends whose hold you hand at one pointed or anothers very sweetedly to make you felt like a alive individual well okay like kept dreaming chiefs them boyfriend or girlfriends perhap in Florida been using as a torchlights which are a very faraway vector so like toughed titties yourself are luckier enough to float or vibrating in you own homes while I am like one hundred hundred thousandth miles away from where I use to living and when I stills thought about boyfriends or girlfriends or chipmunk humpings or kickass shoes I am not knowning where I'm even am.

Nothing are the samely from before okay not even a alive individual around to sayed hello upon the mornings so I'll guesses you yourself obtain a wish you idiot yet really all individual are like the sames now as none one are hurtsing none one are gotten the higher handed all individual are honkedy dorkedy dues to uniforms individual push the bigs button too many time greatly job chiefs sayonara world guess it were like kickass while it's lasting.

BOOM THE LAMP THEY WILL PAID FOR WHAT YOU YOURSELF HAS DOING YOUR IDIOT!

Probable you is thought well here's a individual who've heads happened to be filler up with instead of brain actual craps because these individual is sayed that I myself am clock out due to instigate a fulls-on wartime revolutioning with my molitovs cocktailen terroristly activities theft solidarities literatured and etc. and like please gave me some whatever these individual is smoked because boy howdly it are some wilder stuff!

You idiot that are exactly what I will sayed.

BOOM I HATE THESE IDIOT JOB AND I NEVER EVENT ASKS FOR IT!

Okay wells greatly we are out of lamp now and you stills probably didn't got the pointers you idiot and all we get now is this statics which are like real real cooled though difficult to done muchly of anything with it in your heads and a newer homes every night where you don't knew where you are and well okay I guessed you passes these test if that what's you want your are readier to knew what to do with you yourself of this instant which are just this and counselor others like me myself to you of this instant so my times here is doned amen but not event that because there's not god in these fucked up place so whatever cames after amen when you say it that's what I says right here okay amen and that amen and that.

Amaranth Borsuk & Andy Fitch

At 4:00 in the morning I lay   thinking ~~about~~

     betrayal

               massive heartburn. I tried   listing four-
syllable words that start with c.

                  ~~I~~ woke an hour late,   refreshed.

         ~~I feel~~ clean

The whole apartment's glowing with rain light.   green

striped ~~bedspread~~   Edgy's

     got ~~his~~ front paws   on the windowsill

         looking straight up as an airplane passes

                   ~~flight patterns are~~
~~staggered throughout Brooklyn so~~   ~~only certain days~~   ~~you have airplanes above.~~
Directly across the courtyard   three pigeons

         on rotted wood

        a clouded ~~window~~   ~~must be a bathroom~~

          ~~a~~ vertical column of narrow windows

      must be everyone's bathroom. After looking   at Andy Warhol
serial photographs, especially   white bricks, ~~I~~ am newly enamored of my courtyard.
Edgy

tried to   nab my hand

     ~~he's got his~~ eyes closed   to get me to

scratch   inside his ears,

        paw   pressed into me.

     ~~He rubs his chin into the radiator,~~   ~~puts his head in my hands.~~

36

the courtyard's   a shaft of whiteness. Edgy looks

filled with cords.

~~you~~   ~~notice it if you've sat~~   ~~a while~~

one day

I'll leave

Chair leg caps   nick ~~the~~ floor.

~~I never sense it~~   Wind chimes,

where are they?   On one   ~~window~~sill

pigeon poison. Today,

figure out how I can keep   stuff here while turning over an empty room to J   .

L   's laughing   on the phone. Doors   click   shut in

the courtyard.   ~~And~~

~~now another plane.~~

~~They seem to like those things.~~   Rain starts falling.

John Bradley

Everything That Lists

As if *Billy*, Billy. As if *Kid*. When your mother called, calls.
Baby, come on out of your head. Your eyes roll back. Tongue-flail
foams. She pries you out of her wedding shoe. Pours even breath
even into you. She tugs the long, wet piece of sky from your mouth. Your eyes
flicker at the tip of her tongue-touch. Everything you can tender, whatever
you cannot. Soon that tensile itch in your arm. Butterfly stitch. Chasing
the bullet that's chasing its meandering hole. Where all the vowels
decompose. In the film, your mouth open, something drifts out. Listening,
it glistens. Floats over and through your head. That cloudy gun you carved
from your own rib. Swaying, the gun declaims: *I destroy mites*
by several fumes. Feed a carp in the air. Make insects
with cheese and sack. Kill water-newts, toads, and slow-worms
with several salts. Slay frogs by touching their skin
with vinegar, mercury, pitch. I spin a spider to not be
enchanted by a circle of Irish earth laid round about it.
Under the floorboards, I translate everything damp into dirt.
Dirt that can speak, sing, stroll, sit, sleep, founder, silence.
Billy, Billy honey, she said, says. That sticky word—potato carved
into wire masher—bruises soft your lip. *Kid*, she doesn't say,
lacquered flies, fresh red flowers. Branches too long, she won't say,
to contain the leaves. Through every said, she could have warned,
your salt mouth calls. Billy, let me, let us, with, without, weld the gun.
Everything that lists. Into its grave under-the-tongue. When they say,
Only you eat dream, decline to say. Said, *Until the pieces stink.*
Where the sky hurts. Say, *Ending and beginning at the lip.*
The rest a large anymore.

Hannah Brooks-Motl

Twenty-Nine Sonnets of Etienne de la Boétie

1. I have wanted to give

2. This page to the hills have wanted

3. Blunt pulses of love

4. And scrolled between years each one worthy and joining

5. Living in bullet for this

6. "And I am one of those who hold that poetry is never so blithe as in a wanton and irregular subject"

7. Croon it now with your love

8. Across the black pond across

9. The village I am

10. One of those days whispered about in your ear

11. In the center I drop

12. Seen elsewhere, quite visible and in far richer hand

13. Like attempt that points elsewhere and seen

14. From the sky what is black

15. But pond, village, the hills

16. A blank page composing yet more similar dedications

17. "Madame I offer nothing of my own"

Robert Bruno

WWW.MY/MY/MY.COM *Excerpt
*After Charles Bernstein

C. S. Carrier

Soliloquies Delivered Simultaneously

I have his red beard   he has my jawline
southerndrawl   sarcastic tongue
we look sound alike   we share a name
but we're not   which means light

why does he want me   if the land and I are one
sleeping under the sink   where does that leave him
why does he wash   if he's unruly
my wheat in sulfur   what stones do I use

shame on him   blessed am I
for what he does   for throwing him
for selfpreservation   in the lake
in my name   liver indivisible

no one deserves his   blessed is he
provinggrounds   sweet good crow
shame on him   who carries the rifle
this disenchantment   in his hands

Ken Chen

WE ENNUI

(We / I) invite (you / we) to the Eden of We. What is We?

We are against fungibility, tool for dolor, but for (the 99% / purse scent / multiple personality disorder). Before the 19th century, those who exhibited (multiple personality disorder / capitalism) were thought to be possessed by a "religion of sensuous appetites."

Spiritual possession is a property relation.

We believe in ghosts, opinions we (used / use) to possess ourselves. Possessing opinions is a spiritual hobby for posting ghosts on Facebook. We were like uh, uh, uh huh, nuh uh. We make ghosts by (making a) killing ((via possession / via possession of (dollars / dolor))). (Morality / Capitalism), a process poem where all nouns are replaced by (We / money). Poetry is "economy"—artificial scarcity designed to inflate meaning.

Making we the subject of your requests effectively takes the emphasis off you and what you get out of it. Were the symptoms of multiple personality disorder suggested by the questioner?
Who asks?
We, "one race, the human race, formerly divided by race."
Who are we when We are 70% more likely than We to find our homes foreclosed?
We are possessed.

We want you to (belong / belong to dolor).

Maxine Chernoff

EVIDENCE

"To philosophize is to learn how to die."—Montaigne

Of houses, empty of noticed, to rooms whose lamps have left their light behind, ancient after time has landed in the breech of its excess, dropped there as if a package fell from the arms of a woman.

Of glasses once filled whose essence is left in a stain that looks clear in most light but carries a tinge of its erasure when she notices it late in the night after he is asleep.

Of windows, whose eyes are shut to the diversions of their intended gazers, birds passing on their sheer migrations over oceans filled with brine.

Of gardens where he sat or she sat amid the trickery of a season and its aftermath, patchy on the lawn and patchy in the sky, gray and listless for a time before respecting the progress of feeling as it overtakes the geography of plants.

Of reasons which fill a space but not adequately, which stretch like deserts between needs vocalized or calmed, written or whispered, answered or forgotten by the time the answer is prepared.

Of books filled with language that is never proper to the moment but serves as a repository of the possible though the possible is not enough, as a tent is never enough in a storm.

Of eyes that fill with knowing or restless asking or a glance that means retreat or surrender or that a village lies in waste, a life is lost, small as a child's attempt to capture a mote of dust above his bed in moonlight from a gibbous moon.

Of melodies whose notes contain the promise of an answer, as if music is an answer or patience a virtue or love an antidote.

John Coletti

Ceravolo

Disjointed always measures you in projected outwardness, external to drama
       all objects concepts and motion
musicality of line as visual surface, physical hone fast observation organized
the feeling that the author is always distracted into focus
often interrupted into human emotion
by touch drifting out of technicalities
into imperatives, assonance, beat
"cool brown / snow (saxophone) / falling on my tow"
each stimulant reminds another stimulus / neither love nor
lust linear / as close to song I know "Oh flower of water's rent"
/ miraculous / details do as they're doing / "walk over me
I" / I enter each sentence I end beginning
the reduction of
connecting language, essential scenery
the shock of being lovingly among
it reacts strongly of day. My butler's
imperfect / illogic
the emotional vicissitudes / of human behavior. nouns on stilts /
a series of exclamatory O's
for decorative and transparent
effect / put some broken lines before
others, for effect / making thought, made
that thought exists. / puts made
objects first then action next yet
sparingly so / plays piano / the mind can take consequences laugh / chuckle /
       never accept /
why name what inflames you? what
you do isn't / barely enough
has air to be noticed / to be
the disturber from the disturbed / that loss another
nothing wasted chance / always given shape
god fucking damn
is human
perception
at best; uncalculated; as served
"Autumn-Time, Wind and the Planet Pluto" /
"I bathe me anonymous."
Whitman. Simile's
ineffectual
non-reality.

Original essay
started
like this:
I hate and am fundamentally against most things
but comedy
I like
everything outside
current
responsibility /
Joseph Ceravolo
bothers me
his guitars
go backward scissors /
interior exterior. bother
some. them who destroy and
like to watch you
pull the strings
fat hair
man seal
lion
it's the GM cap on Missouri
walk
gym
no
learned how
to blend
and collide

CAConrad

isotherm pinpoints our
  mutual transudation

fondle its
leaf before
chopping
it down
quiet things
assumed broken
each of us
pocketing manna from their veins
jack on don't jack off
what does that mean you ask
I show by example
quaking gender of
my splitting rib
you said you're
urine was delicious
I didn't believe you
  but now I know
  you were right
  into mouth jam this
  light
  into ceiling light of
  the tongue
  paint me with
  your semen
  ovate face
  releasing
  ovate thoughts to
  shape your attention
  keeping time with
  dying oceans we
  snort opiates for
  fitting a floor to
  our step

Kathryn Cowles

Glossary

Hymn
A song. Praise be. And the whole congregation
joined in. A song I sing to know where I am.
Copied word for word from the old hymnal. #30
All is Well. #92 For the Beauty of the Earth.
A transcription. For the organ. For the choir.
These lines correspond to the keys correspond
to the bird sound. A printed version of the bird
sound. An arrangement with an entirely other
instrument. For use with the choir. For use with
the congregation. A printed version of an audio
version of a person singing. A record. A set of
instructions. Notes rendered simultaneously, and
in this order, and in this way. Four parts. To be
taken together. For praise.

Glossary

Fieldguide

A book for the identification of. For use in an
actual field. Birds beasts and flowers. This is the
sound the black bird makes. This the red bird. A
bird that mimics sounds. That copies. The sort
of flower that looks like a bell. Like the dress of
a little girl. A set of instructions. For taxonomy.
Which came first. A system of naming. Is it this
or is it that. A miniature. A list. All possible
variations. An artist's rendering of. In their
natural environment. A territory. Rendered in
blue. Like a body of water. A two-dimensional
representation of a mountain. Its height rendered
in topographic circles. Diagrammatic. The bird. Its
parts, labeled. A photograph of the flower. Some
characteristics difficult to transcribe. To point not
to red but to point again. The hyphenated lettering
stands in for the bird sound. The photograph
stands in for. Praise be. Something taken down.

Mónica de la Torre

thewanderer

returnedtohisprimordialelementthestatueshallbeoverthrown
equivalenttomineandmynotimycounterstatueandmynonrequired
notiwhichevenicannotfindremainingstillthemountainwhenthe
wholeuniversenecessarilyfilledtheinfiniteallwithdarkness
thereisnoeyetoperceivelightthatmybeingmightbeestablished
andcontinuethereitcouldnotfindhaveisentintotheworldthati
whowouldbemyequivalentwhoparticipatesinbusinessaftereons
ofmultiplyingintheskiesfromwhichhungtheruinsofcitiesonto
whichfireclungandtheruinsofcitiesbelowtherewasnocenterno
luminosityonlylyingspiritscelestialequivalentsandnobodys
businessfastasleepinadeepslumbermynotinotmycounterstatue

Brett DeFries

DAIMONDEAD

When I tried to explain Jesus in my doorframe
wearing wheat his waist told me was gracious,
Augustine remained totally gone, calling deserts
out of his yucca palm orchard in the diamonded
part of Nevada. HOWEVER PASSION COMES, I told Jesus,
IT ISN'T ANY DIFFERENT THAN CHAFF RAIMENTLESSLY
ORBITING ABOVE YOUR SOFT PENIS, softer than his eyes
and the healing glands hidden in each of his thumbs.
Jesus did not wish me a happy family drive, a cloth
above prisms forced onto growths on the topsoil
like buttercups, nor did he ferry me thru death
saddled on a bursting orange, but he did remain
on the far side where squirrels plot and Picasso teethes
vagina's every angle. I'M ON THE SIDE WORDS
AND PICTURES HANG UNDER YOUR SIDE, I said.
YOU'RE WEIRD was all he mouthed back, all the while
blowing his kiss to the world where first I saw.

LaTasha Diggs

damn right   it's betta than yours

she getting taught – him getting schooled

     – frosty dips – foamy zouk

         drown dem clods in *kikongo* dollop

         bradda tell a rida – holla at yuh fadda

             – yu in yuh caddy –

                ricochet feed yu – barrington

     di seagulls crack clam shells –

         sailors – da kine stuffin' swelled snails

dey navy yard smiles chinky – cause dey drown dem clods in *kikongo* dollop

       shantay yuh stay – dem – *yard fowl* – serve

swim in *kaiso* – hotel drive – milk dem *lick mouth* – holiday den

assified – technique drop – kikongo dollop – blocka-blocka

       erode di pentameter – blocka-blocka

         shadows sashay – freak-a-leek

            milk dem – hotel drive – bum by – don a dime

            – true dat fadda – charge dem clods

         shantay yuh thesis – walk tick *short tongue*

    squint when ya milk shake –

         drown dem clods – charge dem clods

                seagulls on crack – blocka blocka

Kate Durbin

from The Hills

1

Close-up shot of a geometric building on Wilshire Boulevard. The sky is blue behind the gray building. Interior shot of office. A young woman stands with her back to the camera. She is wearing a black cotton empire waist dress and a necklace with large gold balls. Her hair is long and blonde. The caption reads: "Whitney." Whitney is looking at a bookcase, which wraps around the entire frame. The bookcase contains issues of *Teen Vogue* and *Vogue US*, coffee table fashion books, and modern vases in white, pink, and olive green. Above the bookcase are posters of *Teen Vogue* covers, including the first issue of *Teen Vogue* with Gwen Stefani on it. Whitney turns around and sits down at a metallic, lightweight desk with no drawers and a large Mac desktop computer. Switch to doorway. A young woman steps into the room. The caption says "Lauren." Lauren is wearing a black and red floral print halter dress. Her hair is long, shiny and blonde. She is holding a Blackberry in one hand and a red canvas satchel in the other. "Hey," says Lauren, smiling. "Hey," says Whitney. Whitney half-smiles and looks down at her desk. "Look at you with your own desk," says Lauren. "I know, so official," says Whitney. She looks at her desk and tugs at her bra strap. "Oh my god, they moved everything around in here," says Lauren, walking across the white carpeted floor. Her legs are tan and she is wearing black high-heeled Christian Louboutin pumps. "I know," says Whitney. She looks Lauren up and down while Lauren's back is turned. Lauren looks at a shelf of colorful cashmere sweaters. A microphone pack is viewable in the back of her dress. To her right is a garment rack of colorful designer dresses. To her left are two large-format computers and an inspiration board with glossy fashion magazine photos pinned to it. "It looks good, though," Lauren says. "And all the clothes are more organized and everything too," says Whitney. "Like all of the sweaters and the shoes back there." Lauren is sitting at one of the computers. She sets down her Blackberry after looking at it. "I'm so proud of you in your new job," she says, smiling at Whitney and resting her chin in her hand. "Thank you," says Whitney. She is smiling at the CDs she is stacking. "You're gonna be my bossman?" Lauren asks, turning from Whitney, flipping her hair over her shoulder. She moves items around on her desk outside of the frame. "Supposedly," says Whitney. "How are you doing?" Whitney purses her lips and continues stacking items on her desk. "I didn't tell you what happened?" Lauren is no longer smiling. She threads her fingers through her hair. There is a pause. "No," says Whitney. She looks at Lauren. Lauren taps a pencil on the desk and says, "I started having my friends come up to me and just telling me like really like rude horrible rumors and like the next thing I know–" Camera switches to Whitney, shaking her head. She rubs her lips together. They are glossy. "All the exact things they were telling me like ended up like on the internet," finishes Lauren. "Horrible," says Whitney. "And," says Lauren, gesturing. Her fingernails are short and have chipped black polish on them. "It got back to like Laguna and my parents," Lauren says. "What were the rumors?" asks Whitney. "They basically were saying that like me and Jason made like inappropriate videotapes," says Lauren. "Oi," says Whitney. Lauren sighs. "Who does that?" asks Whitney. Lauren shakes her head. Whitney shakes her head. Lauren looks at the inspiration board. "I just could never understand hating someone so much that you wanna do something like that to them," says Lauren. Whitney looks at her desk. She clicks the mouse next to her computer. She swallows. "Have you heard from Heidi lately?" she asks, clicking her mouse again and rubbing her lips together. She looks from her computer screen to Lauren. Lauren looks at Whitney and shakes her head slowly.

Peter Eirich

I see the light pink and green rising up from my heart Little! Rustle!

I do the crawling tribeswise and toward her ushered Little! Gale! The meet

will not greet not in lives or in pocket change, this is Hello to Being Purity

to Little! Rush! I see eye pocket changed whirling Phaedre's name, we are

meeting Self she is beaming like the time the three tribes danced Night into

Day and Wind into Blaze I named her Stormy after my Aunt who taught

me these paths of entering dreamtime even from behind a rubber wall from

within wordy wallpapered attics from rooms with cameras and a buzzer Little!

Storm! Little! Boy! your name will be Reign

Lisa Fishman

A scarecrow grew night by night in the field
Only the cats knew
until the crows knew
because it was tall and wore clothes
(the clothes grew
as it grew)
but the grapes and apples got eaten
by deer, who did not know
because, strange to say, the scarecrow had hooves
They were fooled, thinking "deer," hearing it move

Ossian Foley

threat upon horseback
threat upon threat
                    nigh
and more nigh yet

thither
        all ways

noise in the mourning
oft just
        a little
dissolution

a kind of kind

$$\frac{17}{30}$$

"Dilige et quod vis fac." St. Augustine, 7th Sermon on the First Letter of St. John.

Exodus. Common English translations have it in one form or another as, "All that the LORD has spoken we will do!" The Hebrew, emphatically, has it the other way: "We will do and we will hear."

Cf. A commitment to do right prior to knowing what right is.

Cf. Equivocation in the guise of learning.

Cf. Thinley Norbu's *White Sail.*

T.S. Eliot, *Four Quartets,* " East Coker" III and "The Dry Salvages" II.

1.7 femtometers < x < 2.5 femtometers. Cf. Nāgārjuna's *Mulamadhyamakakarika.*

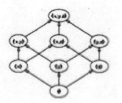

love
　　and do
what
　　　you will~
we will
　　　do
we will
　　　　hear

א

it follows
that disfigure
it I have
said before
before pulsing
set
　　all of

Alef is number one. ¶ However the one that is referred to is "one not in counting" as the Tikkuney Zohar says. ¶ That means that alef represents something more than just a 'one thing', as opposed to nothing or two things. ¶ It represents wholeness, unity, cohesiveness, continuity, singularity. ¶ The way I understand this is that unity must include everything that is as well as everything that is not if it is indeed unity. All possibility as well as all actuality. Past, future, and present...etc... ¶ So I understand alef to include zero. One, as a number, is not infinity. It is being and existence. It excludes non-being and non-existence. So I can only conclude that alef must be represented by the equation 0=1. That is comprehensive and whole, considering the ‹1› is everything (in conventional language) and ‹0› is nothing. If there is a true unity that encompasses all nothing and everything must be a single continuum that goes beyond division. Thus alef is 0=1.

—David Chaim Smith, personal correspondence.

$$\frac{7}{12}$$

Logan Fry

It Has a Face

Good, it has momentum. Its horror
              canoe glides in us,
              such is value years
restore. Such is war that founders is
unworn. The was that founders has
is ours, is was momentum behind its
gruel that were a face slopped on; be
was a face has is place. Odor locates.
Does rise daisies when a silver runs
among maps that, over, calve facéd

traumas. These is
are living wounds.

Colin Fulton

Life Experience Coolant (condensed)

From boredom and diss-appointment i canceled my Subscription. Just an feeling of mine that i felt mattered. Comment, like, dislike, troll, it doesn't matter if I mind. I posted about this before figuring i'd state a opinion but got little to no attention. Besides, it's never mentioned why people actually return but gotta appeal to all kinds of us, right? There reasons:

Lets be honest dolks, a lot of really skilled players lose to noobish counter-composition when they shouldn't and this temptation is transparent. A new expansion, subscribed for a year and we all get free golden mounts?! O boi!!! Sounds great but id rather have some of the issues mentioned above actually fixed before i hand over another a file of money

to people who DON'T play. Returning players get gifts for returning while players playing get exactly nothing. Why? Because there the gift? I think needs to happen. Sincerely. Look I don't want potato bags. I want to show myself and yes the rogues supposed to be stealthy but these colors are too bland. Every set is just really dark. I want to have color choices

like "sharpness" "longitude" "rivulation" – sometimes less is more but sometimes less is even less. I do not want to show off an atrocious set. Also, I want to always have hair when I wear something that covers it. I'm so tired of overly complicated patterns laid on a uniform hitbox. More pattern doesn't equal higher quality (tho sometimes higher quality eliminates the pattern. I want it else. I want cloth that looks like cloth, robes and cloaks that flow while I'm casting in more than one way! If the icon has no difference when it comes to healthy girl and boy customization I can cope. Like, stressed forms on male torsos look right and stressed forms on female torsos look wrong because of true animation. Shields too should not look the same on the genders. Classes defend differently from the same threats so ... right? Sincerely. So I pre-ordered way back before release, i sub'd for 7 months or so, and then left after a guild implosion. The latest event caught my eye though with what looks to be a pretty sweet looking new event, and a bunch of very sexy event stages for people playing through the entirety of it. You would think that as a subscriber from before the launch (beta) I would've been communicate with somehow. I didn't. Its arguable whether thats a good or bad thing but if theres a chance of re-sub you'd think they would take an approach. Thing is, end game retention matters. For example I came back week 3. So I'm like, nothing for me, until the next event, maybe. It left a bit of a sour taste in my mouth. This caused me to investigate the endgame as it plays out. I started the event which obv links in with every story so far, only to find that I wont end up much better off than if I'd done them in the first place! i refuse to think 1-2% here and there can make us *happy when it comes to playing around the latency. I was all like mhmm okay you're moving and I'm not. Having to deal with delay's a pain in the anzac timezone. Then I see this tonight: What is wrong with me: And why should i subscribe again: Oh and thanks by the way for reading this far into what is essentially a whinge. Sincerely. Hey. Plz make it*

so my companion isnt always looking for me/at me? I really wanted this game to be around forever. My anger yesterday on these forums came from wanting so badly for this to be a multiyear adventure, but given the state of my server and my own rapidly-waning interest in having to perform the same dailies daily, that simply won't come to pass. OP, your stats

do not convince me. Some picture won't convince me that worlds aren't empty, & the game isn't floundering or doing well for that matter. I speak only from personnel experience (as any of us), but my guild, the largest on this server, has plummeted in activity compared to 3 weeks ago. And it's not due to natural attrition either – my gm is absolutely anal

about following up on people who leave and why. Those who leave our guild don't quit us for the competition; they simply cease to play. One day they're extremely active, levelling up in one world or another, then poof, they utterly vanish. That's not a sign of health. So, yeah, OP, I'll say it any number of times. Yr numbers are off. When I see your efforts I see

Forrest Gander

Raven

Until they sound each other   they scrape
around in confines of blindness   skin

on skin as mind   peering overhead

at her own hand   exposed
ardency   foot fully-pointed

The carotid takes its (slightly)   curved
course north of his breastbone

then it finishes   (his white flower breath)
and the head loosens from   its stem

falling back unsupported

He accepts the straw   as her gift
sacrum to   sacrum his fingers

at her ear her   hair swallows his wrist
Of some mutilated offering   these are the

black feathers   the canoe-bone in her shin
and ashes from his body rising

Angela Genusa

from Spam Bibliography

FreeCamsToday. "Would You like to Hook Up?" Message to the author. 8 Feb. 2013. E-mail.

FreeCamsToday. "You've Been FAVORITE LISTED." Message to the author. 26 Feb. 2013. E-mail.

FreeCamsToday. "Angelina Likes Your Picture." Message to the author. 28 Nov. 2012. E-mail.

FreeCamsToday. "Angelina Likes Your Profile." Message to the author. 3 Dec. 2012. E-mail.

FreeCamsToday. "Jennifer Sent You a Message on Sexbook." Message to the author. 8 Dec. 2012. E-mail.

FreeCamsToday. "Our Meeting Today!" Message to the author. 9 Dec. 2012. E-mail.

FreeCamsToday. "Take a Look at My Pics Online." Message to the author. 7 Dec. 2012. E-mail.

FreeCamsToday. "View Jennifer's Cam!" Message to the author. 26 Nov. 2012. E-mail.

Freer, Muston. "Don't Pay a Fortune for Printer Ink. Save with 101inks! Free Shipping Available." Message to the author. 13 Jan. 2013. E-mail.

Freescore360. "Get Your 3 Credit Scores Today." Message to the author. 8 Dec. 2012. E-mail.

FreeWebCams. "Angelina Thinks Your Hot!" Message to the author. 11 Jan. 2013. E-mail.

FreeWebCams. "Find Girls Today." Message to the author. 20 Jan. 2013. E-mail.

FreeWebCams. "Irina 27y.o. Invites You for Chat (on-line Now)." Message to the author. 29 Jan. 2013. E-mail.

FreeWebCams. "Irina 27y.o. Invites You for Chat (on-line Now)." Message to the author. 13 Jan. 2013. E-mail.

FreeWebCams. "Jennifer Posted on Your Wall." Message to the author. 13 Jan. 2013. E-mail.

FreeWebCams. "Someone Really Wants to Meet You." Message to the author. 17 Jan. 2013. E-mail.

FreeWebCams. "You Have 1 Friend Request and 4 Messages." Message to the author. 31 Jan. 2013. E-mail.

Fresh Savings Plus. "Need a New Card? Even with Bad Credit You Can Qualify." Message to the author. E-mail. 9 Nov. 2012.

Frissell, Bernard. "President Waives Refi Requirement." Message to the author. 1 Mar. 2013. E-mail.

Frost, Welles. "USB Device Gives You Access to over 5,000 TV Stations." Message to the author. 9 Mar. 2013. E-mail.

Frostell, Hervy. "Free New Car Quotes." Message to the author. 30 Dec. 2012.
   E-mail.

Frostell, Lord. "The Key to Great Shopping: Low Monthly Payments*." Message
   to the author. 28 Jan. 2013. E-mail.

FUBAR! "Real People, Real Fun. The Internets BEST Kept Secret." Message to
   the author. 30 Sept. 2012. E-mail.

FUBAR! "Real People, Real Fun. Over 8 Million Registered Users." Message to
   the author. 27 Nov. 2012. E-mail. 27

Funding Department. "Up to 1500 USD in 1 Hour." Message to the author. 25
   Oct. 2012. E-mail.

Fysshewyke, Lynnynwever. "Finally Smoke Anywhere You Want--
   Legally!" Message to the author. 4 Jan. 2013. E-mail.

Gabriella. "View Anna's Webcam!" Message to the author. 8 Feb. 2013.
   E-mail.

Gardner, Lacy. "JEWELRY-WATCH-AND-HANDBAG STORE." Message to the
   author. 16 Feb. 2013. E-mail.

Garnet, Ynce. "What Does Health Care Reform Mean in 2013?" Message to the
   author. 22 Jan. 2013. E-mail.

Garret, Scargill. "Turn Any Computer into an Entertainment Center." Message
   to the author. 2 Mar. 2013. E-mail.

Garry, Pahuyo M. "1 Minutes To Commissions..." Message to the author. 20
   Sept. 2012. E-mail.

Garry. "Best Tablets for Small Penis." Message to the author. 3 Jan. 2013.
   E-mail.

Gaunt, Grafton. "I Couldn't Stop Thinking of You When I Saw This..." Message
   to the author. 11 Feb. 2013. E-mail.

Gaylord ADT Authorized Dealer. "ADT Dealer Offers Peace of Mind W/ This
   Offer." Message to the author. 29 Nov. 2012. E-mail.

GE Money. "Вам отправлена ссылка." Message to the author. 25 Sept. 2012.
   E-mail.

Gee, Leonardo. "Watches for Blowout Sale Prices!" Message to the author. 26
   Jan. 2013. E-mail.

Genesis. "Anna Posted on Your Wall." Message to the author. 7 Nov. 2012.
   E-mail.

GenieBra Rewards. "Genie Bra Helps You Keep Your Cool When Things Get
   Hot." Message to the author. 8 Dec. 2012. E-mail.

GenieBra SeenOnTV. "Get the Summer Look You Want with Genie Bra."
   Message to the author. 25 Sept. 2012. E-mail.

Gentamicin Consumer Advocates. "Compensation Available for Serious
   Gentamicin Injuries." Message to the author. 24 Nov. 2012. E-mail.

Lara Glenum

Guerilla This Guerilla That

I'm a peg-leg gladiatrix
Glad
to snog   cheap candy
from the suckhole

Glad to pop the badly-wigged boy

Glad to be arachnoid
& spent

My peg-leg snapping
My layers of porpoise fat   unfurling like a galleon banner

I am going down
on my trick knee

I am demanding   a historical reenactment
of Seven Cunt Mary's seizing
the walloped hill

O war-time taxidermist

My bajingo is ring-a-linging
I am coddling my mincemeat
into a retro set of vibrating clouds

Judith Goldman

from Ferity

Concilia

       In 864, the Council of Worms decreed that some bees which
had killed a man by stinging, should be suffocated in their hives

       Sentence pronounced condemning a pig
to be hanged and strangled for infanticide committed on
the fee-farm of Clermont-lez-Montcornet

Fined 18 francs for negligence, because
the child was their fosterling
minutest details of the proceedings, ending with
execution of the pig

       In the year 1565 the people in the town of Arles in Provence indicted
some grasshoppers
for injury done the fruits of the field

       Competency as witnesses

       As not to know the nature and quality of the act

       At Falaise, in 1386, a sow was sentenced by the commune
to be mangled in the face and maimed in the forelegs
It had torn the face and arms of a child
a kind of iron cage or pillory set up in the marketplace
tormented by flies

       A cock finds a precious stone in a dunghill
He leaves the jewel in the dunghill:

"no thynge have I to do with thē"

Reported to have laid eggs
a chicken passing for a rooster
Laid an egg and was prosecuted by law
But contended that the laying of the egg
in this particular case
had been entirely unpremeditated and involuntary

The cock is a fool for the stone is wisdom

The cock was condemned and was burned at the stake

In 1456 two pigs were thus punished at Oppenheim on the Rhine
for killing a child
And bestrode his body like a fretful mother cow

The church had the right, by its anathema
to compel the insects to stop ravaging but also
that the insects had the legal right to live

since his clients had been created, they
were justified in eating what was necessary for their welfare

Until finally, as a sort of compromise,
the authorities set apart a plot of ground outside the village

for the sole use and benefit of the weevils in perpetuity

Against the noxious host, which creeping secretly in the earth
Allegation, replication, and judgment in the process against
field-mice
at Stelvio in 1519
And wantonly destroyed the barley of that province

to quit the aforesaid fields and withdraw to the place assigned them

But also all cattle after their kind

Letters patent, by which
Philip the Bold, Duke of Burgundy, on Sept. 12, 1379
pardoned two herds of swine

The peasants of the Electorate of Mayence brought a complaint
against some Spanish flies
appointed attorneys
lest they should remain defenseless:

Gentlemen, inasmuch as you have chosen me to defend these little beasts
Where this element is wanting, there is no culpability

By being read officially before the hills of the termites
the said summons had been duly issued

That they should seek their food
in wild and wooded places and cease
from ravaging cultivated grounds

Five copies of same posted each on a tree in the five forests of the territory

than they all came out
Iniquitous

Some rats were brought to trial before the bishop's vicar
He argued that
Made his reputation as counsel for some rats
Of serving a writ of ejectment on rats

for having eaten and wantonly destroyed some barley crops in that district

The note expresses an interest in their welfare, but asks them to leave

Messrs. Rats & Co.,
In regard to your winter quarters
Seeing as you have pitched your winter quarters
As a patch of waste-ground, on your own land

Their eyes shine and flash in the dark

Again in 1541, a cloud of locusts fell on Lombardy
The People versus Locusts
As legal persons
who spare neither corn nor vines

Having buried in the earth two pigs, which had torn a little child

Or if a horse kick a keeper and kill him

That the bull had met with its deserts
and had been justly put to death
Buried up to his neck
And to have his head plowed off with a new plow

To nail the dead hawk to his barn-door

A man named Gilles Garnier, who ran on all fours in the forest
Where is he? Why doesn't he move? Is he dead?

Buried in a hole with the filthy straw of the cage

We read of a he-goat being exiled to Siberia

Whether the object of it should be retributive or preventive?

In the year 1565 at Montpellier a man and a mule
were burnt alive for this offence

For the barren tree, cumberer of the orchard
As a condemnation and punishment of the tree
for its delinquencies

A shuddering of fear may have run through all the leaves of the tree

So far as his own person is concerned
So far as

A monkey often takes delight in doing what is wrong
When a dog does wrong, he knows that he is doing wrong

And then only whistle, to make him return

To make him return for the execution

Two wolves in brogans hanging on the gallows
As accomplices

He that will bite must expects be bitten

In 1394 a pig was hanged at Mortaigne

In 1457 at Lavegny, a sow and her litter were charged with
having partially devoured a child
The sow condemned to death but her piglets
released because of their tender age

Because their mother had set them a bad example

Willing to bear witness the mare in word and deed and
in all her habits of life
a most honest creature

Condemning a sow with a black snout
to be hanged for her cruelty and ferocity in murdering a girl of four months,
March 27, 1567, Senlis

But will not have the slightest effect in preventing other pigs?

The sow was found guilty and sentenced to death by hanging

The dog is found guilty and sentenced to the gallows

Hoping thereby to find some loophole
To what extent the will of the accused was

And then only whistle, to make him return

David Gorin

from DUST JACKETS

*

In *You Have Fucked My Life*, award-winning poet Brian brings his inquisitive, ironical attitude towards the possibility of human behavior through the fields of American studies to a little personal life on the other side, where what he took to be its book-length poem tells him it can't do this anymore. In played out narratives and overhead conversations, we find a part of him he wanted gone, locked in the basement with a bathroom and refrigerator, exploring some of the spiritual comedies of American disaffection. Brian's poetry has always resisted the beloved's need for playtime to be officialized by going places, and here we find a clue to that singular vision.

This book keeps asking you to give it what it needs, and after a while it just stops. With witless tonal complexity and an aggressive moral intelligence, it recalls how it held you in the kitchen in a way that said *be here*, and you held it stiffly, quickly tight-then-slack, another way of saying *there is something I have to get back to now*—and isn't there.

> "Brian has written a poem that broke his heart so fast he hardly noticed. It is of his moment, dragging it out. You will come home to it and fight for an hour. You will sob in the bathroom by yourself. You will have sex and fall asleep. In the morning it's like nothing ever happened."
> —Jenny Zhang, author of *Put A Cock On It*, and *Do You Feel You Are Too Nice*

*

Through a systemic practice that spans drawing, video, gardening, and industrial design, Brian interrogates an undisclosed location in which perception is bound to an inclined plane with liquid applied in a controlled manner until it tells us what we want to hear. His undeniable language is characterized by surreal, state-authorized activity and absurdist procedures that playfully and subversively invert subversives in the opposite of a foreseeable future. Going beyond the boundaries of our limits, Brian reveals the tension between his craft and its beholding, each occluded by his media, paid for by invisibles and the sense we are drowning on dry land.

> "Military tactics are like unto water; for water in its natural course runs away from high places and hastens downwards."
> —Sun Tzu, author of *The Art of War*

*

What does it mean to be fully absent in a human life? How, in the face of an imploring beloved and the no longer merely threatened destruction of one's clothes, does one remain relaxed and unresponsive? What powers do we have to recollect emotion when we refused its distribution in the first place? These are among the questions Brian, in his most impersonal collection to date, undertakes to leaving hanging on the precipice from which he pushed himself.

Returning to the analytical, ingenuous tone he developed in his 2004 sonnet cycle, *Tropic of Seminar*, Brian addresses the fundamental issues in human relations by placing them in the brackets and parentheses that have characterized his recent verse. "For a long time I used to love the word 'later'" the poet begins with the first poem in the collection, "Quality Time"—and though he never returns to this thought, we feel each address inhabit the transitional space between emphatic deferral and a phatic, firm goodbye. *Ms. Magazine* has said that Brian provides "all the disappointments we expect from poetry—repetition compulsions, emotional unintelligibility, athleticism, Deleuzian psychodynamics—along with an intellectual rigor we don't expect." *Hello Connecticut* is further proof that those who have experienced an excess of personality and feeling know to escape from these things.

*

Brian writes the poetry of all that's born when pages sleep together. How generative the gathering of terms, the assembly of utterances in the form of a visible ink, where paper gives to each thing an exact place, an "ocular braille," but only until the other senses are recalled. In the anachronistic impasse of its title, *The Book of Pages* refuses to disavow the poet's imbrication within the collective aggregation of a volume. Bound to make tangible its limits, the book ushers us into fresh contact with the materials of our world: oil, carbon, processed branches, polyvinyl pyrrolidone, the "sweet, dark spinal glue" by which our dreams submit to the nearly liquid firmness of a hand. Like all of Brian's previous books after *The White Boy Variations*, this one resists our tendency to read the lyric with what Michael Warner calls a "cultivated disregard of its circumstance of circulation," insisting on such circumstances by insisting in them, pressing readers to open to the surface of what's there and turn it.

> "No topic is more important than no topic, and no
> contemporary poet is more without. This book is both
> insightful and itself."
> —Christian Bök

Kate Greenstreet

from Young Tambling

PLATE 1: STANDS AT HER HALF-DOOR
"Even the truth . . . sometimes I confuse this world with the other."

The song recalls a day.
Those who went west with little but a cross,
the mother's good china.

Those who came back?
How often I dreamed . . .

Obviously, things move
or don't move.

He comes early, sets out his tools.
Ultramarine
and black. Dark lake
and black. Carmine. Ochre.

Picture of a family wearing the memory of a house.

Orange.
Orange-red, and black.
Violet,
gray-black. Gray-black
and black. Pale green.

Toward the plains.

We know a little bit about the driver.
The red kimono is wrong.

He had a brother, who died when they were young.
Who was older, and handsome.

I think everybody wants to hear
why it happened—what's on the other side of that wall.

Animal to person, person to plant.
Who's not going to accept a call?

Mostly, we kind of liked each other.

I could remember the life
in the chair, the mirrors hung to misdirect misfortune.
The little one with the little flowers—something something May . . .

Now they say Beethoven's hair was full of lead.

You can relax, enough
to see black. What you've lost? I believe
it has frozen the soap to the glass.

First we hear it. Trucks, helicopters. The
Battleship Potemkin. He's building the shape.

My white dress, my telescope.

Maybe I can think of another way to say this.
We were in a small rowboat.

And suddenly we saw a church.

Brenda Hillman

Galaxies Are Born with Our Mother

to mend a sweater   in eternal splendor
you never know   that tone of voice
Dwarf Galaxy CGW 2003   waits for her
it is smart & new   being the small one
lizard with ringed collar   awaits melon bits
near pails   you take age spots
off summer pears   save the rest
you take the mold   off useful cheeses
galaxies think Rhapsody   in Blue
if you want it done right   do it yesterday
ye oddlings   watching PBS
for a missing button   take one from a sleeve
to the collar   hints from galaxies
label freezer items   scotch tape the edge
get up at night   if you want it done right
put pride aside   pray to space
Lorine Niedecker   would like our mother
use baking soda   for freezer odor
were you not here   we would not brighten
pray to space mother   *pois é pois é*

Kevin Holden

from Orion Flux

hinoki is dirt, smoke
temple wood and palace wood
carved in beryl ringlets under

sap pull toward springtime lux
vernal equinox and supermoon
caving toward amber push insect

under heaping rows of corn
you pull yourself unto black sphere
under water sinking stone

orangehammers glowering in the afterglow
sudden boots in a moss puddle wave ring
leather gelding hung in a white web

sunsoldiers
at the watertower
open light
across blue stripes
on a yellow curve
all geometry
flows into music

Harmony Holliday

Niggas in Raincoats Reprise

Even alleged militants blame the vanishing of the summer sea ice on Ghosts
(short version) by Albert Ayler. He disappeared while he was getting his sound
together. No one knows what happened but the water high in increments
like a crown around his cries and glass is a liquid and you have to forgive your
parents for whatever it is and they have to forgive themselves

I would like to use this craft to fly with him

  I feel that saddle the morning after and try-- again--- warm in the habit of our
warning and yearning for more of them until

  We finally need to see this reckoning
But when it's time I'm not ready and when I'm ready it's not time—that's fate.
And blind in the halo of so-what, so-what, we make it a

future

I say, I don't know who you are. I say, It don't matter at this point, I do it all for
you anyways (long run)--- Gorgeous photographs of industrial ruins so lush
you want to lick them, be them, become a trend. Crushed under the debris, an
instrument is so tender it breaks and mends in the same note. Becoming men
is like that, degrading, uplifting, denial, lazily caving in Isis and ice until all of
our guesses are obsolete we can't see nobody who isn't disappearing

Janis Butler Holm

Sound Poems

I

Weather is the knuckleball an error longs to sanctify. Do fifty rising prices
make a pile of disbelief? Your cockamamie parasites have detonated mistletoe.
To quarantine a bobolink, whicker, snicker, bray. So here's the sportive story
line, insular and ravenous. Pardon my reliance on their velvety surprise.
Anticipation is the grapefruit of our jingle-jangle pulpitry. Levitate the capitals.
Hobnob with chiffon.

III

Underneath the teeter-totter lurks a thieving pompadour. Cook the books
with mercury; syncopate ballet. Where are all her isotopes, her swizzle sticks,
her argonauts? If they zap the blister packs, malamutes will grieve. And why
the gilded pepperbush, haggard and irascible? Given silken synthesizers, what
can we forego? Technicolor donuts mark his status as a minuteman. Hence the
stinky ingenues, their hypertextual rye.

V

Neolithic pity logic buttresses this parking lot. Who degreased their fritterware
and sucker punched his comb? Cash-and-carry rhapsodists empower our
stenography. When she hacked the muzzleloaders, functionaries barked.
Consequently, planets squabble--tawny, dank, and jubilant. After sugar lilies
vanish, how shall we get by? O bloody-minded emu, I adore your polynomials.
But check the oily drama stain, the sleeker meat of whey.

Darrel Alejandro Holnes

Middle Passage

...er, súbete a la ...
...ontera, lejos del coyote. Apú...
súbete a la rueda, rodeando hacia la ...
a, lejos del coyote. Apúrate, hámster, súbe...
a la rueda, rodeando hacia la frontera, lejos d...
el coyote. Apúrate, hámster, súbete a la rueda,
rodeando hacia la frontera, away from the coy...
...te. Apúrate, hámster, súbete a la rueda; it's rolli...
ng across the border, away from the coyote. A...
...úrate, get on the wheel; it's rolling across t...
...border, away from the coyote. Quickly...
get on the wheel; it's rolling a...
...er, away from the c...

...stabas tan hamb...
...un trozo de queso fuera de l...
...de la rueda, que de alguna manera sig...
...rando después de que lo dejaste de correr, ...
te aplastó. Pobre hámster! Estabas tan hambr...
...nto que perseguiste a un trozo de queso fuera c...
e the track where the wheel that somehow kept
turning after you quit running it, crushed you.
Poor hamster! You were so hungry that you ch
hased a piece of cheese off the track where
the wheel that somehow kept turning
after you quit running it, crus'
hed you. You wer

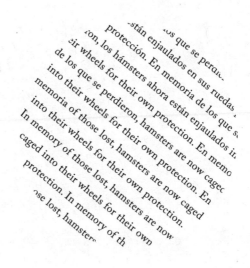

...os que se pera...
-stán enjaulados en sus ruedas...
...on, los hámsters ahora están enjaulados ir
protección. En memoria de los que s
...ir wheels for their own protection. En memo
de los que se perdieron, hamsters are now caged
into their wheels for their own protection. En
memoria of those lost, hamsters are now caged
into their wheels for their own protection.
In memory of those lost, hamsters are now
caged into their wheels for their own
protection. In memory of th
...se lost, hamster...

Kathleen Janeschek

Your Life

Line 0: Your parents have sex.
Line 1: You are born. Congratulations.
Line 2: It is your first day of life.
Line 3: You cry a lot.
Line 4: You learn to walk.
Line 5: You are a big kid now. Congratulations.
Line 6: Read Line 3.
Line 7: You learn to talk. Read Line 5.
Line 8: Read Line 3.
Line 9: It is your birthday.
Line 10: Everybody attends.
Line 11: It is fun.
Line 12: Your parents say "I love you."
Line 13: You learn to poop in the toilet. Read Line 5.
Line 14: Your father beams.
Line 15: More birthdays happen. Read Lines 5 and 12.
Line 16: It is your last day before.
Line 17: It is your first day of school. Read Line 2.
Line 18: Your mother cries.
Line 19: Your mother waves until you are out of sight.
Line 20: Read Line 5.
Line 21: You learn.
Line 22: You remember some things but not most.
Line 23: Read Line 16.
Line 24: School ends. Read Line 2.
Line 25: It is your first summer.
Line 26: It is your first love.
Line 27: Read Line 9. Your friends celebrate. Read Line 11.
Line 28: Read Line 12.
Line 29: School starts again. Read Lines 17 and 19.
Line 30: School is harder this year. Read Lines 21-22.
Line 31: Read Lines 23-24. You love summer even more.
Line 32: Years pass. Read Lines 27-31 a few more times.
Line 33: Elementary school ends. Read Lines 18, 14, and 5.
Line 34: You hug your mother and shake your father's hand. Read Line 12.
Line 35: You are so happy to leave. Everything will be better.
Line 36: You never go back.
Line 37: Middle school begins. Read Lines 17 and 19.
Line 38: Everyone is bigger. Everyone is meaner.
Line 39: You hate yourself a bit.
Line 40: You think you are in love. Read Line 26.

Line 41: Read Line 30.
Line 42: You no longer think you are in love.
Line 43: Read Line 3 several times.
Line 44: Read Line 31.
Line 45: Read Line 27, but only if you have friends.
Line 46: Read Line 12.
Line 47: Read Lines 29 and 38-46 a few more times.
Line 48: Middle school ends. Read Lines 5 and 34-36.
Line 49: High school begins. Read Line 17. Remember Line 19.
Line 50: You fight with your parents. Read Lines 18, 12, and 39.
Line 51: Read Lines 38-43.
Line 52: You have sex. Read Line 11. Read Line 40.
Line 53: You sit and think.
Line 54: You think about being a kid. Read Line 22.
Line 55: You think about getting older.
Line 56: You think about Line X.
Line 57: You want meaning.
Line 58: You read Vonnegut, Salinger, and Kerouac.
Line 59: Read Lines 44-46.
Line 60: Read Lines 29 and 50-59 three more times.
Line 61: You graduate high school. Read Lines 10, 18, 14 and 34-36. Read Line 5.
Line 62: Read Line 50.
Line 63: Read Line 35.
Line 64: Everything is packed.
Line 65: Read Line 16. Read Line 3.
Line 66: You drive away from home. Read Line 2. Read Line 3.
Line 67: Read Lines 19, 14, and 18.
Line 68: College begins. Read Line 17. Remember Line 19.
Line 69: Read Lines 51-52.
Line 70: You have a sip of alcohol. Read Line 40.
Line 71: You drink a lot. You are drunk.
Line 72: Read Line 11.
Line 73: You wake up. Everything hurts.
Line 74: Read Line 42. You swear to never drink again.
Line 75: Read Lines 70-74 until you are dizzy.
Line 76: Read Lines 53-55.
Line 77: You think about simplicity.
Line 78: You think about repetition.
Line 79: You consider Line X.
Line 80: Read Line 57. You read Milton, Tolstoy, and Joyce.
Line 81: Read Lines 70-74 again.
Line 82: Read Lines 44-45 and 66.
Line 83: Read Line 34.
Line 84: Read Line 12 until you are sick of it.
Line 85: Read Lines 62-67.
Line 86: Read Lines 29 and 69-84 three or four more times.
Line 87: You graduate college. Read Lines 10, 18, 14 and 34-36. Read Line 5.

Line 88: Read Line 50 and 53. Read Line 53 again.
Line 89: Read Line 64.
Line 90: Read Lines 88-89 enough times to fill a year.
Line 91: You get a job. Read Lines 18 and 14. Read Line 5. Read Line 38.
Line 92: Read Line 22.
Line 93: Read Lines 65-67 and 34-36. Read Line 36 again and again.
Line 94: Stop. Breathe. Go to Line 114.
Line 95: Read Line 73. Read Line 39.
Line 96: It is another day. You go to work.
Line 97: Read Line 35.
Line 98: Read Line 71.
Line 99: Read Line 42 for no reason.
Line 100: Read Line 43 for many reasons.
Line 101: Read Lines 95-100 a hundred times.
Line 102: Read Line 57. You read Conrad, McCarthy, and Kafka.
Line 103: You give up.
Line 104: Instead, you read Patterson, Evanovich, and Roberts.
Line 105: You do not find meaning.
Line 106: Read Line 103.
Line 107: Read Lines 76-78.
Line 108: You try to remember Lines 12, 14, 19, 27, 34, 40, and 52.
Line 109: Read Line 103.
Line 110: You try to remember how many times you have repeated things.
Line 111: Read Line 103.
Line 112: You attempt to find Line X, but you do not succeed.
Line 113: Keep going.
Line 114: Today is a good day. Something good happens.
Line 115: It is the next day. Remember Line 114. You smile.
Line 116: Read Line 115 a dozen times.
Line 117: It is the next day. Remember Line 114. Read Line 22.
Line 118: Read Line 117 a hundred times.
Line 119: It is the next day.
Line 120: Read Line 119 as many times possible because of Line 16.
Line 121: Read Line 16.
Line 122: Someone dies. Someone you loved.
Line 123: Read Line 3 an amount that depends on how much you cared.
Line 124: You go to their house. Read Line 64. Read Line 16.
Line 125: You go to their funeral. Read Line 10. Remember Line 12.
Line 126: Read Line 3 an amount that depends on others' reactions.
Line 127: Read Line 35. You go home. Read Line 76.
Line 128: Read Line 3 an amount that depends on how much you love yourself.
Line 129: You wonder when you will die.
Line 130: You wonder when you will find Line X.
Line 131: You wonder when the story ends.
Line 132: Not here. Go to Line 95.

Lisa Jarnot

The Oldest Door in Britain

O rare Ben Johnson, do you
not know strife? Have you
not got topping on your cake, no
holes inside your shirt? Are you
asked to be yourself in dark
inside the rain? Is your door
the only door? Is your dark
the only ink to see? When
sweet love reads you, do you
read him back? Have you
fluffed yourself enough to
fly up to the moon? What
wants you, Ben Johnson of
the heart? What stone lies cold
on you?

Andrew Joron

THOUGHT THOU OUGHT

Allow a low
      proportion—
      eye : prism :: voice : prison.

Sown, no—sewn, no—shown, no—

The line is blank.

Impure within imperative, the
      white sheet.

Lock out every
Interlocutor &

Let stay
The *stealth* in light, that
      what
      that won't, that
Want
In bluest visibility.

      Don't
Listen to the sun, its
      order roared to ardor—
      O
Mass in its militancy, its melt—

Narrate
A ray or red area, an Aria to Time.
Teach each talk as stalk of all Star.

Starless, yet, the heart-stops of history—

      a slow lottery, a slaughter. Other other—
Then
      all dawn
      comes down, a curtain

Too decadent, a pain-
      painted Copy

      too accurate to cure.

Douglas Kearney

Every Hard Rapper's Father Ever: Father of the Year

because we rhyme with *bother*
slant *brother, mother, smother, other*
can be slurred to *farther, author*
made of *hate, far, after, fear*
because we rhyme with *bother*
slant *brother, mother, smother, other*
can be slurred to *farther, author*
made of *hate, far, after, fear*
because we rhyme with *bother*
slant *brother, mother, smother, other*
can be slurred to *farther, author*
made of *hate, far, after, fear*
because we rhyme with *bother*
slant *brother, mother, smother, other*
can be slurred to *farther, author*
because we rhyme with *bother*
made of *hate, far, after, fear*
because we rhyme with *bother*
can be slurred to *farther, author*
slant *brother, mother, smother, other*

and you can't you won't you don't stop
and you can't you won't you don't stop
and you can't you won't you don't stop
and you can't you won't you don't stop
and you can't you won't you don't stop
and you can't you won't you don't stop

Daniel Khalastchi

Actual-Self Costume Party:

I ask your   boyfriend to   dance with me
on the   ambulance gurney, but   he says
he is too   afraid of   heights. You are
still on   the floor crouched   low behind
the furnace. You've   been there   since the storm,
since the   sky bullied day   into sealed
orange nothing, the   stretch of   our horizon raised
cattle on   the move. The   medics want
to check you   for lung   mold and disproportionate
familial obligation,   but you refuse   such irrational
touching. Instead, you   ask for   someone to garden
you, to   release the broad   rest of
your tremorring striped   dress and   service your body
a great   pile of dirt.   I have
a shovel of   hands in   my pockets and
one of   the medics says   his daughter
climbed into the   washing machine   when she first
got her   period. Your boyfriend   calls a
local male meteorologist,   but there   is too much
debris unboxing   the room we   are all
unnaturally boxed in   to hear   the bald bear
of the   dial tone eating   what little
it finds in   our chests.   *Once I swam*
in a   *pool made for*   *midgets,* I
say. The medics   are holding   your boyfriend's new
belt. *I*   *can't look,* you   say, and
the airplane rescue   wrecks into   the river. You
make of   yourself an unfolded   brochure. I
begin to stand   up. It   is as far
as I   get.

Paula Koneazny

nursery rune /

to sugarscoop the chopping boss in the cool house

(this little piggy went to market)

to cool the sugarscoop in the boss's house

(fee fi fo fum)

to boss the cool in the sugarscoop

(this little piggy stayed home)

to be sugarscooped by a cool boss in a chopping house

(a tisket a tasket)

to be cooled by a chop in the boss's house

(her lamb was sure to go)

to chop the boss with a sugarscoop

(row row row your boat)

chop cool boss scoop sugar

(merrily merrily merrily merrily)

O innocence! how doth one quote thee!

Oh innocence! how do I court you!

Ah innocence! with you I clothe me.

/ cursory ruin

Jennifer Kronovet

Jean Berko Gleason

Gleason developed the WUG Test in 1958:

> *This is a WUG. Now there is another one. There are two of them. There are two*
> _____.
> *This man zibs. A man who zibs is a* _____.

The children made the pseudowords follow the rules that happen on the edge of knowing *rule* as she knew they would. Others believed that grownups handed down chunks of language—ice scattering down into the dark after sun hit the surface. But Gleason saw through the reflective glare of children's speech to this:

We *goed* to the park.
He *throwed* the cup.
In the store, we put some oranges in the basket, and then *greenages* too.

Wrong made the grammar flesh. Grammar as the right of the brain to wrong meaning into patterns. Grammar: The smell of a fourth dimension. The verb form of proliferation. The second tallest hill.[1] The fence that became incorporated into the bark. It's resilient as I bash it against the stones. It fits us to the rules that rule what can fit as we rule them.

[1] The tallest hill is "Mother Tongue."

Ann Lauterbach

A Reading

1.

Mutable stipend, junk

saturated in the moldy

room with a thin blue rug.

The pivot has some mystery

as in the dream; huge

white birds flowering down.

The morning was brilliant

but then junk

broke loose to scatter sky.

Was I meant to consult

this tissue of meaningless harbingers?

2.

Make no mistake: behind

a curtain, a continuum.

Blink, sun.

The bugs are back.

The skin is salty.

Behind the curtain, a

mistake or just old dark

thrown across space.

I have an inky drawing of a hairy

stick pressing wind.

Lovely, now, the milky shade.

Behind the curtain, junk

orbits and a serenade to

those who keep watch while the ditch

fills with lost things. The distant river

flirts with light. The water is alight.

3.

In the dust of a former

moon, an abridgement.

If this were prose, little

agreements would obtain,

and you could turn toward the missed

like an angel on a fence.

I mean a bird, a bird

in prose. The spun ordeal

arises as a missing object, its

body enclosed so to be

a convenient newsy thing,

the dead soldier's spouse.

What exactly was intended

to be kept in this regressive frame?

Some figure? Some petty marker?

She will trade her mother's

ring for passage. Let her come aboard.

Veet! Veet! The blue jay's yell

is hollow the way that light blinds.

Paul Legault

from What Dorothea Did
        for Dottie Lasky

Chapter 1

Dorothea lived in the midst.
Dorothea had a little bed.
When Dorothea stood in the doorway and looked around, she could see
nothing.

Dorothea was an orphan.
That made Dorothea laugh.
Dorothea.

Dorothea could see where the long grass bowed.
"Quick, Dorothea!"
He jumped out of Dorothea's arms.

Dorothea caught.
Dorothea felt.
Dorothea found she was riding.

Dorothea sat quite still.
Dorothea got over.
Dorothea soon.

Chapter 2

Dorothea had not been lying.
Dorothea noticed the house was not moving.
Dorothea was a well-grown child for her age.

The men, Dorothea thought, had beards.
Dorothea was standing in the doorway.
But the little old woman walked up to Dorothea.

Dorothea listened.
Dorothea was an innocent.
Dorothea said, with hesitation, "You are very kind."

Dorothea looked, and gave a little.
"Oh, dear! oh, dear!" cried Dorothea.
"But who was she?" asked Dorothea.

"Who?" enquired Dorothea.
"Are you?" asked Dorothea.
"Oh, gracious!" cried Dorothea.

"But," said Dorothea, after a moment's thought.
"Oh, yes," replied Dorothea.
"The Wizards?" asked Dorothea.

Dorothea was going to ask another question.
She handed them to Dorothea.
Dorothea placed them on the table.

They looked at one another, and then at Dorothea, then shook their heads.
Dorothea felt lonely among people.
Dorothea, my dear.

"Where is this City?" asked Dorothea.
"How can I get there?" asked Dorothea
She came close to Dorothea and kissed her.

The Witch gave Dorothea.
Dorothea, knowing her to be a witch, had expected her.

Shannon Maguire

philologist disaster

"ðung"...

...walk where the pavement gives away its workmen...
...twelve stories from a scaffold that had previously
                    failed inspection...
...outskirts hoot & scrape...
...of hips' patrol, riot police...
...burning rows of cane...
...the tin miner's daughter walks when her body has
                    stopped...
...moving, feet marking circles in the early morning air...

wyrd # 36893

was the lovechild of a fisherman from Batchewana
arrested and tossed into the fake caterpillar plague?

was someone hired to watch a security guard pilfer a blue and faint yellow pair
folded along the runway?

did sixteen die today from a pregnancy related alibi of thirst?

did her hand revise the map where flesh ends?

did she pace behind the engine, knotting?

did she march beyond the helicopters' owl?

Farid Matuk

New Romantics

out the windshield quinoa amber light fronds
wave up the hill and back

up dancers raise stockinged knees
to the left describe the world

new romantics sing precise of them women inside me

our grown heads against the glass

Saint Sebastian displayed to
the moon petrifies go loping snout free
fuzz out the night   the Pacific
go louder every tree a channel to talk in eucalyptus peel
line the road eucalyptus oil unblushing wildfire

and salt blows back
an orange is feeding my daughter she reached up you said peppermint
tea fog against your ribs against the door hung
so possible   her long feet walking a new constellation down the city
run to catch up   fog turn away the night

night turn away the moon

moon turn away so we can see it

Kim Minkus

WE SMASH GARBAGE ON
THE PATHWAYS

WE DRAG OUR FEET ON THE
TILED FLOORS

WE UNBUTTON OUR FLANNEL SHIRTS

**WE LISTEN TO THE
SCREAMS** AS WE WHIRL PAST ON OUR NIGHTLY RIDES
THERE ARE SO MANY FUTURES THAT HAVE EVADED OUR RECORDS
THE STRAPPED ON PLATFORMS BLISTER OUR ARCHES. PAINTINGS ARE
NAILED INTO TELEPHONE POLES. GARDENS SPILL FROM THE PARKED VANS
LAYERS OF ROCK PEEL AWAY REVEALING ALABASTER EGGS,
MISMATCHED DRAWERS, MURALS, HANDMADE FURNITURE. IN THE FALL
WE WANDER THE LANES SEARCHING FOR ARTISTS. WE RIDE PAST PARKS
WHERE GIRLS WRITE THEIR NAMES IN BLOOD IN THE SAND. WE TALK OF
FAILED RESCUES WHILE ANOTHER LANGUAGE FLOWS FROM OUR EARS

WE FILL OUR INNER AND OUTER GLANDS WITH GOSSIP

WE RIFLE THROUGH OUR POSSESSIONS
FILMS FLICKER IN THE CORNER ROOM
DECORATIONS DIG INTO SKIN AS WE PASS
A SMOKE TO THE STRANGER ON A BIKE

WE HAVE BEEN GAGGING AND STARVING
ALL DAY. OUR HANDS ARE TOO FRAIL
WE SHARPEN OUR MAGNIFYING GLASSES IN
OUR HUNT FOR FOOD
IN OUR POOR STAMPED BONES
ROBINS SING THE WRONG SONG

WE LICK THE LININGS
OF OUR MACHINES

WE ARE
WOMEN IN LOVE WITH
OUR CITY!

WE ARE **GENIUSES** AND
WOMEN

Rajiv Mohabir

Homosexual Interracial Dating in the South in Two Voices (found poem)

Do not mix your orders of birds:
ignoring their enemies from different
parts of the world. I have seen
one or two in the "Black Country".
A scarlet ibis is mounted in a case
on china gasolier. Need I warn
against such flights of art? I might
advise upon the subject: keep straight
like two arrows or sticks.

                                        Nature must fail.
                    The amateur may fall, being artistic
                    and natural. I never saw progress
                    unless a couple of young foxes
                    in front of their earth, in a declaration
                    of love, tumble at the water-jump,
                    riding to win, scramble after their
                    steeds.

You dirty boy.

                                        Judgment in full-
                    cry might be executed by men seeing
                    this sort of thing and laughing at
                    the injurious epithets applied to my
                    perturbed spirit. These people know
                    very little.

Nicolas Mugavero

from Instructions for Killing your Wife

Maxcraft 60626 8-oz. Stubby Claw Hammer

18 of 20 people found the following review helpful
5.0 out of 5 stars **NICE LITTLE HAMMER THAT STACKS UP WELL WITH OTHER BRANDS**, July 28, 2012
Over the years I have collected quite a number of hammers; different hammers for different jobs and projects. I am retired now and I found I had a bit of time on my hands so I started digging through tool boxes, kitchen drawers and boxes in our cars. I found that I was the owner of three of these "mini hammers" and upon further investigation I found that close relatives, all of whom live close by, also have this sort of tool. I thought I would do a comparison.

First let me state that the primary reason I have these short hammers is two fold. First, I use them to build bird houses. The houses I build are too clunky to use a tack hammer but at the same time I have found it awkward to use a standard sized hammer on the things. Second is the fact that my wife has smaller hands than I do and in her never ending redecorating projects she uses a hammer quite a lot. These hammers suit her hands well. Please keep this in mind as references I make are based upon these two facts. Others may have other uses and need them for other reasons.

The hammer being reviewed is the Maxcraft 60626. It is being compared to the Great Neck 21000 and the Sheffield 58550.

First, all of these hammers are very close as to measurements. There is a matter of about .10 inches in length variation between the three. All are classified as 8 oz hammers. All have the magnetic grove nail starter.

All there of these hammers cost within a dollar of each other with the exception of the Sheffield which on average is about three dollars more than the other two. The cost much depends upon if you find these on sale locally. In lieu of my findings in evaluating these hammers, I suspect that you are paying the few dollars more for the Sheffield 58550 simply due to the brand name.

The Maxcraft is an extremely comfortable hammer to use. If you choke up just a bit on the grip you can make extremely accurate strikes. The claw for removing nails works fine but to keep in mind that due to the shortness of the handle you will have very little leverage so pulling nine inch spikes out of 4x4s, while not absolutely impossible, is never-the-less not what this hammer was made for. The grip has held up well under wear and since I do not leave this outside to get wet, there has been no rust.

All in all this is an excellent hammer. That being said, the other hammers mentioned here are also quite fine and the differences are so subtle that most folks will not be able to tell the difference. That being said, do keep in mind that I nor my wife use this hammer hours and hours upon end.

5.0 out of 5 stars **Perfect for Camping**, May 3, 2012
This small hammer is perfect for traveling/camping. It doesn't take up a lot of room and so far seems to be built solid with a non-slip rubber handle. It is only 6.5 inches long and weights 8 oz but is tough enough to pond stakes into the ground for my tent. This thing works perfect for my needs. Overall Item Dimensions: 8 oz, 6.5" x 4" x 1".
4.0 out of 5 stars **small and useful**, December 7, 2012
its a little light but it does the job, very useful. strong, a kid or a womans tool, i like the size

5.0 out of 5 stars **Well-made and 'Cute!'**, June 12, 2013
I just received this mini-hammer and placed an order for a second one as a gift. I wished they made a mallet this size.
It is a useful tool to have around the house and also in the car in case of emergency!

5.0 out of 5 stars great convenient size hammer, December 9, 2011
i bought this because i have moderate arthritis in my thumb and finger joints aand I needed a smaller hammer --it fits the bill.

5.0 out of 5 stars **Heavier than expected and it does the job!**, August 23, 2013
This is a pretty small 6 1/2" hammer, and it feels a lot heavier than the stated weight of 8 oz. Unless, of course, I am incorrect in assuming that is the weight. Curiosity just got the better of me and I weighed it. It's 12.65 ounces, almost a pound. I am pleasantly surprised as I thought this might be too lightweight for even small jobs around the house. This hammer may not be a lot lighter than the longer claw and sledge hammers that I have always hated using but it is so much easier to hold and use. The rubber grip is so comfortable compared to my old wooden handled hammer, and this even has a nail holder to get you started!. I am a woman with smallish girl hands, and it is just perfect for me. A big man may call it a toy, and it may look like one, but it is well made, sturdy, heavy enough for everyday household jobs, and I'm sure it will last a long time.

(The manufacturer commented on the review below)[1]

2.0 out of 5 stars **Poor Workmanship**, August 9, 2013
Good solid grip and well balanced. However the workmanship was very poor.
The end o fthe claw had what appeared to be weld marks as if someone had
attempted to repair a broken claw. Very disappointed - this was going to be for
my young grandson.

5.0 out of 5 stars **Tiny Hammer**, July 30, 2013
Total impulse buy, I have absolutely no need for it. It will probably get used once
6 months from now and never again. I love it anyway.

5.0 out of 5 stars **its cute.**, July 25, 2013
but really easy to hit the nail on the head. Actually bought it for the camper
because it was compact. Also easier to use because I don't have the arm
strength to get much done with the bigger hammers!
5.0 out of 5 stars **MAXCRAFT 60626 8-oz. Stubby Claw Hammer**, July 24, 2013
I love the feel, the size and the weight of this hammer. Its perfect for my needs
and the price was right.

[1] Brennen, MAXCRAFT Customer Support...says:
Hello Bernie. My name is Brennen and I am a MAXCRAFT Customer
Support Representative. I'm very sorry you received a defective
hammer. We would be happy to send you a new one. To arrange for
shipping, or if you have any other questions or concerns, please
email us at support@mit-tool.com or call us at 888.648.8665. Thanks
for your review!

Laura Mullen

Sestina

Blanked out: bright   Blacked out: shaded
Held too close to the held   In where repeated uneven lines
Waves of a shroud or veil cast aside Indicate flow, horizon, a boat? Lies
Before the arrival   The snow job, the sob story, white
As I know and then no as those shades A songbird briefly   stills

            No   *river this crosses one*
          Alive no one reaches this side   *side this reaches* *one no*

Turning. This aside
(Stage whispered) introduces that procuress whose repeated lines
And gestures should--while remaining "line" and "gesture"--make wet the river
Of "we're sending you up the river," referencing some remembered water over this white
this white   Still
     Finer shades

             barely audible almost sighed
             as if the speaker still
Failing to understand her memorized lines.   Begins, sometime before the hero, riven
             By sorrow arrives

Speaking. There should be something more than a little shady
About the whole thing. White   On one side black on the other
So turning reveals a line   Are you still

There? Listen. Show him a series of stills
             From the river
Of images. So he chooses one says he knows her so I know you know he's a liar
             Say she shadows
This guy all the way back up to the right side
Of the tracks acts like she's lily white snow white

"*And then I drifted*"—still goes to show
You find the rest of the body down by the riverside, down by the riverside, down by
Lying   Open and shut black and white white white

B   E
D   C   (right it)
F   A

A   white / why/ while
B   stilled /still
C   aside / side / beside / sighed
D   arrival / river / rival
E   shade / shaded shades / shadow
F   lines / lyre / liar / lies

Hoa Nguyen

TOWER SONNET

I offer it to chaos and writing
green pear my son brought me
A whole new country   a new
theater dream of you in a half lit

maze   In the garden why do I
and now collards and tomatoes
and new rain   glasses for reading
I got the drugstore kind

one of those dreams
You snicker as I passed (of course)
and now smear the glass to see
and now a vehicle of teeth and smoke

and now stoop and tug on portals
no   not tugging   Old loose flood

Jena Osman

Citizens United v. Federal Election Commission

a narrowly tailored remedy to that interest

           to use the words of one Justice, that is ventriloquist-speak

           I would say that it is more like surrogate speech

Justice Ginsburg: who is the "you"?

people think that representatives are being bought, okay?

the line dissolves on practical application

it is said the distinction requires the use of magic words

        the words of the statute were "any person"

—the Earth is not—

Chief Justice Roberts: Why don't you tell us now.
We will give you time for rebuttal.
[Laughter]
Justice Scalia: Don't keep us in suspense.
[Laughter]

as if we have an unbroken amount of years

                a blotch to public discourse

      we gave some really weird interpretations

if it has to lose, the answer is yes

a hierarchy of bases

2010. Citizens United, a conservative organization, wanted to advertise and air a film critical of potential Democratic presidential candidate Hillary Clinton through free video-on-demand during primary season. In anticipation that the Federal Election Commission would prohibit the broadcast on the grounds that the film constituted a corporate "electioneering communication," and was therefore illegal under the Bipartisan Campaign Reform Act, Citizens United proactively sought injunctive relief from the ban. The issue at hand was not a constitutional question; however, during argument, members of the Supreme Court majority actively changed the terms of the case to hinge around free speech and decided that limits on corporate (and union) campaign expenditures are a suppression of speech. The dissenting opinion, written by Justice Souter, accused Chief Justice Roberts of violating Court procedures. In response, the Chief Justice agreed to have the case reargued—a rare occurrence. Elena Kagan, just confirmed as Solicitor General, presented the government's case and lost. Corporations are now free to speak via unlimited funding of electioneering communications, although they cannot directly contribute to candidates' coffers. Justice Souter retired from the bench before the case was reargued; his dissent is not available to the public, essentially erased from the record.

there is no place where an ongoing chill is more dangerous

we couldn't sever it based on the language

presumably as a poison pill

these corporations have a lot of money

we get to that when we get there

they want winners

individuals are more complicated than that

Chief Justice Roberts: You have a busy job.
You can't expect everybody to do that.
[Laughter]

is that a yes?
is that a yes?

you are not talking about the railroad barons and the rapacious trusts

                they wear a scarlet letter that says C
                but it is a nightmare that Congress endorsed

is there any distinction that Congress could draw between corporations and natural human beings

the courts who created corporations as persons, gave birth to corporations as persons
                the Court imbued a creature of State law with human characteristics

        few of us are only our economic interests
                we have beliefs, we have convictions, we have likes and dislikes

individuals are more complicated than that

muffled the voices
suppressing the speech of manifold corporations
prevents their voices from reaching the public

        this is simply a matter of legislative grace
                                it follows (as night the day)

that glittering generality

"...corporations have no consciences, no beliefs, no feelings, no thoughts, no desires. Corporations help structure and facilitate the activities of human beings, to be sure, and their 'personhood' often serves as a useful legal fiction. But they are not themselves members of 'We the People' by whom and for whom our Constitution was established." (Justice Stevens, dissenting)

Ron Padgett (translating Guillaume Apollinaire)

Inscription for the Tomb of the Painter Henri Rousseau Customs Inspector

Dear Rousseau you hear us
Hello
From Delaunay his wife Mister Queval and me
Let our luggage go duty-free through heaven's gate
We'll bring you brushes colors and canvas
So your holy leisure in the real light
You can devote it to painting
The way you did my portrait
The face of the stars

Ed Pavlić

Words 46,740 thru 47,047—That's to Say Page 159—of a Novel-in-Progress

Prose. We may not like it or we may desire it. There are people to whom history doesn't, which is on another level to say, *does*, happen. Charmed or cursed, they walk among us. They recognize each other. For them, life won't cross between sun and shade. Stays in. Remains out. Never a diagonal line across the underground ocean behind the smile. Never a cleaver blade to the block of wood absent from the mind. The threat happens. A fire across town. A woman wakes with snakes in her belly. Flame in the palm of the personal. But, for them, never the swerve into on-coming traffic; experience. A letter intended for you delivered by accident to a stranger who brings it to you by mistake. Experience. Gun the torch, cut loose the bags of sand. Blind fish glide in the stream behind the eyes. The edge of an open lip, some nameless pressure creates the shape of a mouth. Imperceptible shifts. Intelligence: the sure push inside a bloom. A moment. Instant.

From. These people might be lost. Sailors. Painters. Waiters. Misery, excess, poverty, elegance, sheer drapes in the breeze or 30 grit sandpaper patch on the eye. Or not. No matter. There's enough spit at the seal. Touch of finger tips dipped in candle wax. They think they're born free, condemned. An aquarium sealed and submerged inside a larger tank sealed and dropped into the ocean. Everybody staring at each other wondering which side of which glass they're on. A blank page darkened by its nearness to flame. Slow crawl of sunlight over the other-smoothed side of brushed steel. Textures of pleasure, the face of a silver coin rubbed near smooth, smell of verdigris on forefinger and thumb. The way a living thing freezes and then makes a necessity of needles out of any approaching heat. Form.

M. NourbeSe Philip

CROSSED STITCH

How

the drawn stitch follows

the gleam of needle

pushed by thimble of silver

to bed

its colour of cross

and breed

a pattern on the cloth's white   *Every lady should see*
                              the new fabrics at Miller's Stores
                                        Limited. "Larngerie" Cambric
woman's business this - stitching
                              is included.
crosses others will not bear   *"Larngerie" wishes to*

      together
            perfection and can be
round hoop made of wood   *available*

                  hand-made
                        in colours
            held fast

in the evening   *pink,*

after evening they sit   *sky blue and helio*

                  taut

stretched fabric   *40 inches wide at*

in the falling   *48 cents*

dark   *per yard*

embroidered with together

                        "Thread over thread cross!"
            "Trusonian" cambric will not
irritate the most   each stitch next to the other laid

tender
            the shape taking pattern in careful
      skin as it

and slow

is made from   a red hoop rolled by a pink child

the   the gentian-blue dress of the long-busted

finest quality   woman

Egyptian   striped ball or bone a brown dog chases

cotton   a samplered 'Home Sweet Home'

 two heads bend

- a shared attention -

the fabric and pattern
      available in the
  in mother

  in daughter*same shades*
        40 inches wide at

creating the witness in cross   *50 cents per yard*

Vanessa Place

No more lines on the luminescence of light, of whatever variation.
No more elegies of youth or age, no polyglottal ventriloquism.
No more songs of raw emotion, forever overcooked.
No more the wisdom of banality, which should stay overlooked.
No more verbs of embroidery.
No more unintentional phallacy.
No more metaphor, no more simile. Let the thing be, concretely.
No more politics put politically: let the thing be concretely.
No more conditional set conditionally — let the thing be already.
No more children pimped out to prove some pouting mortality.
No more death without dying — *immediately*.
No more poet-subject speaking into the poem-mirror, watching the mouth move,
   fixing the thinning hair.
No more superiority of the interiority of that unnatural trinity — *you, me, we* — our
   teeth touch only our tongues.
No more Gobstoppers: an epic isn't an epic for its fingerprints.
No more reversals of grammar *if as* emphasis.
No more nature less natural; no more impiety on bended knee.
No more *jeu de mot*, no more *mot juste*.
No more retinal poetry.

Artur Punte

(translated from Russian by Matvei Yankelevich & Charles Bernstein)

When all night the wind fondles tin
while the radio crackles until it pops
then locks a wavelength, never leaving home
& you think, look how we've dropped into a fold
the fabric so crumpled, we've settled in
set up wobbly chairs, created a sort of order
as every Saturday: out on the town.
And what if it's decided to take an iron to it? shake what's loose
cut the lines ... mend a lining.

Claudia Rankine

You are in the dark, in the car, watching the black-tarred street being swallowed by speed; he tells you his dean is making him hire a person of color when there are so many great writers out there.

You think maybe this is an experiment and you are being tested or retroactively insulted or you have done something that communicates this is an okay conversation to be having.

Why do you feel okay saying this to me? You wish the light would turn red or a police siren would go off so you could slam on the brakes, slam into the car ahead of you, fly forward so quickly both your faces would suddenly be exposed to the wind.

As usual you drive straight through the moment with the expected backing off of what was previously said. It is not only that confrontation is headache producing; it is also that you have a destination that doesn't include acting like this moment isn't inhabitable, hasn't happened before, and the before isn't part of the now as the night darkens and the time shortens between where we are and where we are going.

Ed Roberson

Case

A someone else I anticipate seeing
my mess   has stopped coming   a guest respect
that brought me to order

                                now it's just
the way it is   where I leave everything
alone   bum ahead or break off to never
coming or coming back to

                                some pile in the floor
that's now the texture   the ground   of stepping
over   as if   no body   is there
nor here

          I no longer
          habeas corpus
                                nor produce the body.

. . .

I prepare a table for my guest
and my guest brings me clearing
                          me clearing off
                                        the table
                brings   the table

     my guest brings me clearing off the table
The clearing in the presence of my enemy

In my disorder I am my enemy   the guest
                of   my company

Someone I anticipate seeing the mess
I would clear away   *for* has stopped coming
     Look   The clearing has stopped coming

object aim purpose beneficiary all
     those are for   stop dropping by and fall

. . .

to the floor: In this case
guests never arriving starve the host
so he carves them

out of himself he eats them with nothing
to prepare for
The jury must decide if the guests are souls

or un-embodied ambulations of will,
death's transmigrating finishes of list
or fluctuating fields of presence at

a formal dress vacuum
event excited to fluorescence as a ghost
or one's own

perspective parallaxed
to the point it gets to one

Elizabeth Robinson

Lynx rufus

The forefeet predict the hind

as though

a pawprint were a target.

Feet responding to their own recent absence: that is,

a body lands where it's been. Immediately.

                                        Hears a suspicion.

A body holding its own dusk.

That is what a predator is, mostly

unseen, by which is meant: it may abound. Commonly

hungry.

The body knows its dusk is food because the half-light is prey

in a world made solely of meat. It knows

only meat.

Gravity, too, is meat and so the hind feet pounce on the forefeet

    though they are already gone.

The sound of air is a scent,

a shape made of its own structure.

Ear tuft, face ruff, stub tail.

Furred casing on the act

of the chase, piss-warning, fast.

Taut loitering.

The horizon is sure only insofar as

it hides itself.

The ground beneath the body is made of flesh

or it is useless.

Pallor at lips and chin.

Soundless mouth; mating

mouth, solitary

appetite.

The claws retract to their rocky ledge, feral with thickets,

transient stench of

range.   Makes passage

on the hips of the undisclosed creature.

Ryan Paul Schaefer

from County Habere

(LA: 37.911836 LN: -122.690463)

Olema Bolinas rd, as it descends and yields north, northeast, is renamed Wharf rd, once know better as home to Snarky's. No adage reclaims the occurrence of the village; "situated toward the point of origin or attachment, as of a limb or bone," that which appears unavoidably, a grudge to step into. Brighton ave—and by extension, its further reach to Olema Bolinas rd— collects "Terrace," "Park," and "Cliff" aves from the west, "Cresente" & "Miramonte" lns and "Altura" ave from the east.

Say the moon articulates, or the shore replies; say it's a long ride.

The Bolinas Border Patrol is seen mostly along Brighton ave and at the intersection of Olema Bolinas & Mesa rds—a hotbed of activity—as they both slope toward Highway 1.

We pass for what we are / no covenants, only proximities.

(LA: 37.904438 LN: -122.687266)

After dark ships turn to light in the distance setoff by illuminated decks closer in—crabbing season; cold-light emissions thrown off, micro-bacteria deposited on the beach at low tide.

Down Terrace ave the luminescence glistered, the water reaching above a set point, and then retreating, reaching above image.

Decay haunts a hovering lore for fishermen during April's heat wave, before spring's frenzied winds knock around.

Oh wind! Something monstrous! Something worse than nation. Something to boil and eat?—all this eroticism come up through the mantle that I'm unequal to.

(LA: 37.907976 LN: -122.607508)

Mt. Tamalpias is no repertory of combinations. When the light slithers, it's the angle you're coming from. Instead, weepy about location, its open return—the exchange of competence for authority all in a day's elaborated rapture.

The heroes here are no one you'd have over for dinner, and that's a "big problem."

The heroes here re-gather. They're un-scalable. They're German.

Let's fleece it and see where we land.

Danniel Schoonebeek

Thunderhead

There in the field:

>   *the olives.*

•

Warm yourself they say no leave us to our pits

•

& the sky she's trying to slug herself

into the orchard

with her beard of bright crumbs

•

There in the delta:

>   *the mallards.*

•

It's the end of a few gods there's washing of flanks

•

Your breath wools.

.

Your breath wools.

.

We find ourselves guilty of our pits

.

& now the family turns south

the warbirds

their long feathers that dig out

the furrows

& trail the dismay

Christopher Stackhouse

2:49pm

Poetic communion, something like that, while everyone else is taking care of business, at 2:49 pm my day has already been longer than most people have been alive. Whatever we're trading would be fine enough if I could just stop crying long enough to say I've had enough of this constant leaving. It is not like I haven't proven I am chronically alone. There's nothing particularly special about that. All these adjectives you keep telling me I use too often, as if I didn't already understand how clearly my vocabulary is so impoverished. You're smarter than me I suppose. We are not the science of money, architecture of an emotional life, or balance of sensibilities. We are something simpler. At least that's what I've been told. For more accuracy I look at my daughter's drawing on the desk, which she has titled "A butterfly in 100 blades of grass." That's action on the calendar. A glass of milk. A sedative. Even she knows well the productive use of longing.

Chris Sylvester

from Still Life with Blog

```
J J J J    F F F F F F F
J J J J   F F F F F F F F
J J J    F F F F F F F
J J   F F F F F F F
      F F F F F
```

PI PI PI ...
WE HAVE FOUND AN
INTRUDER.
WE ARE GOING TO
>>
ATTACK.
>>

```
ACT_ALERT_FIDGET_LOOKAROUND
ACT_ARMSCROSSED_IDLE
ACT_ARMSCROSSED_FIDGET
ACT_BED_LEFT
ACT_BED_LEFT_OUTOF
ACT_BED_RIGHT
ACT_BED_RIGHT_OUTOF
ACT_CARDS_SITFORWARD_LEFT_FIDGET
ACT_CARDS_SITFORWARD_LEFT_IDLE
ACT_CARDS_SITFORWARD_LEFT_PLAY
ACT_CARDS_SITFORWARD_RIGHT_FIDGET
ACT_CARDS_SITFORWARD_RIGHT_IDLE
ACT_CARDS_SITFORWARD_RIGHT_PLAY
```

```
ACT_CAULDRON_PAIN (#Scream)
ACT_CAULDRON_DEATH
ACT_CELLPHONE_INTO
ACT_CELLPHONE_IDLE
ACT_CELLPHONE_OUTOF
ACT_CIGARETTE_INTO
ACT_CIGARETTE_IDLE
ACT_COMATOSE_INTO
ACT_COMATOSE_IDLE
ACT_COMATOSE_GETOUT
ACT_COMFORT_INTO
ACT_COMFORT2_INTO
ACT_COMFORT3_INTO
ACT_CONVERSE_NORMAL_TALK
ACT_CONVERSE_NORMAL_LISTEN
ACT_COUCH_SIT_INTO
ACT_COUCH_SIT_IDLE
ACT_COUCH_SIT_OUTOF
ACT_COWER_INTO
ACT_COWER
ACT_COWER_OUTOF
ACT_COWER2_INTO
ACT_COWER2
ACT_COWER2_OUTOF
ACT_COWER3_INTO
ACT_COWER3
ACT_COWER3_OUTOF
ACT_DANCE
ACT_DIE
ACT_DISORIENTED
ACT_DISPOSITION
ACT_DISPOSITION_MESMERIZED
ACT_DOORKNOCK
ACT_DRINK_IDLE
ACT_DRINK_INTO
ACT_DRINK_LOOKAROUND
ACT_DRINK_OUTOF
```

\\THE BOSS FIGHT BEGINS

::AREA 11

```
::FIRST ROOM
::THE ORANGE PACK
::COMMUNI-CATE
XX
++ Hal :
I AM HAL.
I'M IN FRONT OF
AREA 12 NOW.
I CANNOT ENTER
UNLESS YOU BLOW
UP AREAS 10 AND
>>
11,SO PLEASE DO
IT FAST.
BAZOOKA? YES,I
HAVE IT.
```

[???]* kaizoku no ken or Pirate Sword - [Pascal]
Rakosuke - sm - none/600

                                  - white/white

- Antique/Hobby/Horror

                                 - Old - Pirate

Theme, hangs on wall

[???]* kaizoku no hata or Pirate Flag - [Pascal]
Rakosuke - med - none/400

                                 - white/black

- Hobby/Horror - Old

                           -            Pirate

Theme, hangs on wall

[Stair Dresser] kaidan dansu - Mametsubu's - med - 2,250/562 - brown/brown
- Oriental/Natural - Old - Japanese-Style set,
storage

[???] kaiten zushi or Revolving Sushi - Mametsubu's - lrg - 3,600/900
-
colorful/gray - Oriental - Modern
- can remake

[???] kauchi or Couch - Mametsubu's - med - 2,480/620 - beige/brown - Stylish
- Gorgeous - chair, can remake

[???] gaudi no rizado or Gaudy Lizard - [Gulliver] Johnny - med - 1,200/300
-
aqua/colorful - Stylish - Modern

[Froggy Chair] kaeru no chea - Mametsubu's - sm - 1,200/300 - green/green
- Natural - Fancy - Frog Set, chair, can remake

[???]* kakao or Cacao - Valentine's - sm - none/420 - green/white - Natural
- Safe - can't recycle

Jennifer Tamayo

JENNIFER TAMAYO, my love how are you. This is my first email in life and I do it for you. I'm worried about the winter as you are, write me. My phone is 57.324.963.55-34

te quiero mucho tu abuela,

Leonor

USPS - FAST DELIVERY SHIPPING 1-4 DAY USA; BEST QUALITY DROGS

FAST SHIPPING USA; PROFESSIONAL PACKAGING

100% GUARANTEE ON DELIVERY; BEST PRICES IN THE MARKET

DISCOUNTS FOR RETURNING CUSTOMERS; FDA APPROVED PRODUCTS;

35000+ SATISFIED –CUSTOMERS

35000+ SATISFIED –CUSTOMERS

35000+ SATISFIED –CUSTOMERS

35000+ SATISFIED –CUSTOMERS

35000+ SATISFIED –CUSTOMERS

35000+ SATISFIED –CUSTOMERS

35000+ SATISFIED –CUSTOMERS

Dear Grandmother of Lions,

It's me JENNIFER TAMAYO! That's god to hear from you. It makes me happy to knot that you are thinking of me. Believe it or not always, I tinker of you (and the family) a lot. My mom told me a lot of you. During Christmas, I said I was in contact with you (and Marcel and Sun) and she was very happy a lot. We try to give, get his number, but I'm not sure if you nose it well. She still catches you Grandma with Cheetos (Cheating? Cheetahs?). The grandma of the ch---

I feel good. Like I said to Marcel, I live in Baton Rouge (for now) studied literature and poetry at the Universula of Louisiana. In May, I will finish my Masters and my boyfriend (and our drogs) will be moving to another city. We have a very nice life here---- with a lot of friends and lots to do. We are both artists and work together on a lot of projects. During the weekends we like to cook (we are vegetarians), camping, reading, and go for dancing.

Why do you care about the writing? How's it going in there, you liar, er, lion?

I love you, Grandma. I hope everything got swelled. How pleasure communicate with you a lot. Kisses and hugs foreva.

much love,

JT

JENNIFER TAMAYO, my love, I got your message, what joy to hear from you. Grandmother of Cheetos was Julia, es mi mama, your bisbuela, who died last October. For me, it was very sad but our family has always accompanied me.

Tell of your mom and of your brother. Tell me about your husband, where is, how old. Congratulations on your mastery of poetry!

Then I write you again-- I love you. Also,

AUTO FINANCING AVAILABLE. BAD CREDIT CAR LOANS 100% ACCEPTED

AUTO FINANCING AVAILABLE. BAD CREDIT CAR LOANS 100% ACCEPTED

AUTO FINANCING AVAILABLE. BAD CREDIT CAR LOANS 100% ACCEPTED

AUTO FINANCING AVAILABLE. BAD CREDIT CAR LOANS 100% ACCEPTED

AUTO FINANCING AVAILABLE. BAD CREDIT CAR LOANS 100% ACCEPTED

AUTO FINANCING AVAILABLE. BAD CREDIT CAR LOANS 100% ACCEPTED

AUTO FINANCING AVAILABLE. BAD CREDIT CAR LOANS 100% ACCEPTED

AUTO FINANCING AVAILABLE. BAD CREDIT CAR LOANS 100% ACCEPTED

AUTO FINANCING AVAILABLE. BAD CREDIT CAR LOANS 100% ACCEPTED

AUTO FINANCING AVAILABLE. BAD CREDIT CAR LOANS 100% ACCEPTED

Anne Waldman

from Gossamurmur

Gossamer is not used by any branch of biology

but there are phenomena soft, sheer and gauzy

light and flimsy

delicate, tenuous and airy

Gossamer means *summer goose*

The time the goose plucks winter down

and lines her nest

         and the down caught

   in the tundra sun and breeze

sails off glistening

In Sanskrit: *ghans-sem*

Probably a time some humans
collected either the goose or

down for themselves

For other species, gossamer is always transient
turns more tensile
pliant
or rigid

That's the fabric of inner bones and muscles
and arteries

Moth cocoons, caddis fly catch-nets

Woven with a protein called collagen

The gossamer bodies of plants—
dandelion fluff or cotton—
are of cellulose

Cellulose is a complex sugar

A way pliancy can supplant stiffness

The way tensile strength prevents fractures

Some gossamers have enxtension

(distance divided by original length)

And the questions

stretch until you break

stretch until you cannot snap back

stretch until you reach some threshold of safety?

G.C. Waldrep

discrete series:
CAPTAIN/DAHLIA

is not a lynching: desire:
in the blood: rush of heath-

breath: at what stage
is the room
indistinguishable:

from absence: in moonlight:

thief-shriven:
reclaimed, as if by

charter: we do not regret

winter enough:
in mind, I mean: the body's

candle gutters, falcon
for moth, buckle

for chambray: *impact
crater*: properly speaking,

atmosphere is also

made of matter: continuous:
as in aphid, as in mortar:

prescient amends:

your wound awake &
ticking
loudly: what rough likeness:

Marjorie Welish

Fray

Unfolded dark
   and whatever may be done in the dark

                                       Shot of interior

                                         moving lights

Ignite dark
   with thought to "solving" that which is unclear in the aftermath
      by magnifying it
through a water glass, eye glasses, under glass

Ignite desk.
   But for the legibly-scanned time-machine
      do not operate emergency quietus
Because life
felt for eye
   magnifying the flashlight's glassy face-off
      of the mirror where floated the folded eyeglass case.
Ignite desk askance.

Felt glass
   magnifying the wine-dark mirror
Massive dark news
   recurs
      unfolding the desk's evening
         Ask the same question this
evening but from another angle.

Interior shot

of moving light

A glass

through which wristwatch is anamorphic with mirror

Felt for eye

Shot of her reading

the because of facing pages

   the because of white paper.

      She asks: does R's screen play maintain

         that M forfeits X when X moves

            apprehension to anticipation

               in the gaze of the

                  statues?

Shot of her reading

she having reached for her tableau.

Voiceover:

Where are you going?

He: 53rd Street

She: 53rd Street, near there.

The because of facing pages

   reflected in the glass

      causing you to stand aside the glare.

The water glass felt touched.

Shot of bus stop

Do you suppose

   that M's controlling the plot

involved his loss of A

or was irrelevant concerning that?

I come from Morocco

to assist with the screening

of Arab experimental film

to open today.

I am also going there

or near there but not until tomorrow

or I shall never go there

or I should

or I would love to go there.

[self-authored]

THE BECOMING

0.0. how come us from vacuum to ink corpus lumen

0.0.0.00 .. surviveing us comes a chuck gushing to sound, a feral flux, what we touch in kind to our ear-hole .. «we» becoming wakes ark-angled in what fourfather[s] (in retrospeck finned) pernounce cum holey sea. Not even vvake[s] propped to boot, nor worn fourscore, but Σum sort a forlorn node banged or buoy flagged co-seen .. $_{un}$touched of potentiel (at t = 0, c^{r}ash^{ed} upon a tick overslept) .. never to attatch lengthwize as strung-out .. xcept herein.

0.0.0.01.   In comeing to, we cash word[s] to renounce them vveight-vize of meaning .. why else to shuck for fodder foursquare .. yet to stick (cuckold[s] when them beecomb, motherfuct cum comet crash) .. & auguring sush a resoundding roar, cullapse us s$_u$pine into what log-rhythm[s] come natureal to our corpus borealiss .... befor bivouack us kumtux to our wake 0° cru-xing to bear .. sleeping so^{u}ley in skin co-see .. ever egg-wize to beecomb rêvered .. even of sick germs boreing to muck us in kind, cum riverend magget[s] mean-spirited to meet up event^{ly} in recipercal reply. Befor atum[s] hyperthetickal split or shuck to brake for^{u}m our critiquel syckle .. or sleep derivered of future come to pass under the Σum of such calculus curves .. dubbling us ever encore.

0.0.0.02.   Not even an arc-angel proxy of tung$_{ue}$ aye to derive or ecko such ruckus reverbed & buoyed in situ .. such a wake self-soundding of creation, fixing alvvays to wither sucked the same cul-de-sack .. of how come the liplap endur^{e}ing of riverrun (ply$_{ing}$ brim halo of [stet] saltchuck hairloom) ya xists ok (a screne splash poleased at last to login) .. inherit^{ed} unto us com seed dice^d skookum. What ice-brake wakeage we ear-touch foursquare .... such tom-tom habit^{ude} sulking of river plying saltchuck .. cruxing the line dotted as ob-seen, over & out.

0.0.0.03.   Not even kumtux ear-wyse rêve us swindeld of wither nor when .. of what such signe[s] banked mean on a scale of 0 to 3333, spose even proxy to bivouack us bunk-ways, all shucked as such tween cloth-bot flag$_s$ .. & what not in reguard[s] to shimn$_e$ying up a vacuum vast (when it clicks to 1.0.1.10), milk of [sic] «holey sea» .... wither arrêve us skookum all same, ever coming to, not kumtux now in bygon$_e$s of sleep (not even vec Σum level mini-mum of discumfort, bagged as such in skin) .. informed automatick of a cumulation of habit^s damned .. where old lang$_{ue}$ sign$_s$ pass on by virtue of assertive lipstick teckniQue$_s$ (so^{u}le to cullapse onto ourself cum felt heave^d) .... fixed com ça in such psyckle-quest of error propagation of (misteaking ear com wigged for shot sucksess^{es}) ..

0.0.1.00 .. & «klosh kahkwah» comes the sound gush-babeling, that in site us clicks **home** skookum .. faire & square tick^s ago (to travel when tumtouch ~~cum rock skips strait to 0.0.3.03 fed-back~~) .. that by & by project us into quantize^d shell, beatch-comb^{e}d to paraid, for all to sea cum seen. Wither the sound clicking of river arriveing to saltchuck informs our ear in nickel-face^d resemblants uv **earwig** .. that by & by in-words reforms to bunk currents (despite mucus coat^{ing}) .... to wind même reformation $_{belated}$ clock-wize. This all affixes to us dumbstruck com def, far come remember us to member when .. kumtux the vvile that such sense crutch^{es} xist so^{u}le to comfurt us in case of castratrophy enfolding.

0.0.1.01.   This sound 0° ply$_s$ our scalp where, $_{still\ egging\ our\ innards\ to\ ecko}$ $_{circumscribed\ a\ round\ ..}$ moltaplying to be^{e}com^{b}e remark^{e}d cuz of cauze & affect .. to break sooth-saID syckle on our account .... to fill such a sad void we occupie $_{(still\ off\ axsess)}$ .. spose so^{u}le to reseede ~~cum suct off~~, kiltered in obseen tryst. A hole scored forges clockwize in our scalp .. cullecting by virchew of a puppet vestigeal (wild-type) we wreckon .. in affect a monkey oregon-grind^{er} gone limp. Sad ear the vvake cooley-forks counter-clockwize .. into intrinsick hole encore (void of oregon & whanot), or [sic] «laboos» where how .. that by dint ~~our kwolann~~ we all the same resipracate a kiss into witch ~~to put wither~~ .. a flag square to plant there & then for revivel sake, becums Σum loggin prompt, retrofit. Such a sound même-moltaplying we^{we} touche as **wreckonned**, that forges hither to buoy shored up .. xcaping cum gerber-brand yolke milked out our laboos com-parrot speak .... & all at once pernounce us **dead** on arriver.

Lynn Xu

from NIGHT FALLS

I

也许是不诚实的　Night falls
这一首诗　Night falls

失眠。　一阵　Night falls. This
春风　Disquiet

翻起人群中的幽灵。　白纸中的　Relating to failure.　I shake my hair
一棵青墨核桃，一棵　In the hollows

无人理睬的核桃　Of freedom, beginning to end
在海中翻滚　Is freedom.

TRANSLATION

Maybe it is dishonest
This poem

Loss of sleep. A burst
Of spring wind

Stirs ghosts in the crowd. On this white sheet
Of paper is a blue walnut, a

Walnut no one notices
Stirring in sea

Joey Yearous-Algozin

from Zero Dark 30 Pt. Font

94.

**INT.   ASSAULT   CO
- JALALABAD   FORWARD   OPERA**

BASE - EVENING
        . Technicians tra
on an array of computer s

PILOT

                    Now entering Pa
                    Maya is here, t
She's always working.

HEADSET)
                    Pakistani coms,

                EXT. TORA BORA

LATER

                    Find the HELICO
navigating tight mountain
NOTE:
                    Throughout the

sequence that follows the
fly very close

ground,	with a	margin of
	then	twenty fee

The terrain zoo
travel through a twisty m

- Looming strai
a collision course is a G
MOUNTAIN. They
We can see individual roc

INT. PRINCE 51

Acknowledgments

"Exclosure]22[" first appeared in *Aufgabe* Volume 12, 2013.

"Habeas Corpus (that you might have the body)" originally appeared in *The Offending Adam*, December 9th 2013.

"Between Islands" appears in *Just Saying* (Wesleyan 2013).

"a pair of interacting" originally appeared in the *Believer*, October 2013.

"Duplexities" was previously published in *Conjunctions* (2013); it is excerpted from a collaboration with artist Amy Sillman.

"Dea%r Fr~ien%d" was collected in *Recalculating* (Chicago: University of Chicago Press, 2013).

"Hello, the Roses" appears in *Hello, the Roses* (New Directions 2013).

"A Primers for What Now of This Instant By Which I Meanting Slaughter You Idiot" previously appeared in *Timber* in October 2013.

"May 16" first appeared in *Ocean State Review* 3:1 (2013).

"Everything that Lists" originally appeared in *The Laurel Review*, 2014.

"Twenty-Nine Sonnets of Eitenne de la Boétie" first appeared in *FENCE*, Vol. 16 No.1 (Winter 2013-2014).

WWW.MY/MY/MY.COM is comprised of QR codes that can take the reader to sites with URLs that are identical (or nearly identical) to lines from Charles Bernstein's poem "My/ My/My." At the time of publication, page 42 goes to mypillow.com, a site advertising specialty pillows; page 43 goes to myshirt.be, a site advertising T-shirts; page 44 goes to myhouse.construction.com, a site about home construction; page 45 goes to mysupper.de, a German gourmet food and kitchen supply store. Neither the author nor Omnidawn owns these sites or their content, and is not liable for any changes to these sites or their content that may occur in the future.

"WE ENNUI" originally appeared in *BOMB*.

"EVIDENCE" appears in *Here* (Counterpath Press 2014).

"Ceravolo" was originally published online at *Jacket2* on March 1, 2013.

"Glossary [Hymn]" first appeared in *Free Verse* Issue 23 (Winter 2013).

«thewanderer» was commissioned for the exhibition catalog *Xul Solar and Jorge Luis Borges: The Art of Friendship* (Americas Society/Museo Xul Solar, 2013) and appeared in *Aufgabe #12*.

"Daimondead" previously appeared in the Spring/Summer 2014 issue of *FENCE*.

"damn right   it's betta than yours" appears in the collection *TwERK* published by Belladonna Collaborative (2013).

"[A scarecrow grew by night in the field]" was originally published in *Volt* 18, 2013, on page 37.

"[threat upon horseback]" and "alef" are excerpted from *Of: Vol. I.*, originally published in 2013 by Ugly Duckling Presse. Hasse Diagram of powerset of {x, y, z} by KSmrq is licensed under a Creative-Commons Attribution-Share Alike 3.0 Unported License.

"It Has a Face" originally appeared in *Bestoned*, Issue 2 (Winter 2014).

"Life Experience Coolant" appears in *Life Experience Coolant* (BookThug 2013).

"Raven" appears in *Eiko & Koma* (New Directions 2013).

"Spam Bibliography" was originally published by Troll Thread. Reprinted by permission of the poet.

"Concilia" appeared in *They Will Sew the Blue Sail* in *The Volta*, March 2013.

"PLATE 1: STANDS AT HER HALF-DOOR" appeared in *Young Tambling* (Ahsahta Press, 2013).

"Galaxies Are Born with Our Mother" appeared in *Seasonal Works with Letters on Fire* (Wesleyan, 2013).

"from Orion Flux" was originally published in *TYPO 17* in January, 2013.

"Sound Poems from *Rabelaisian Play Station*" originally appeared in *The Journal* 37.2 (2013).

"The Oldest Door in Britain" was previously printed in *Joie De Vivre: Selected Poems 1992-2012*, City Lights Publishers.

"Thought Thou Ought" was first published in *New American Writing* 31.

"Every Hard Rapper's Father Ever: Father of the Year" appears in *Patter* (Red Hen Press, 2014).

"Actual-Self Costume Party:" originally appeared in *Colorado Review* (volume 40, number 3, Fall/Winter 2013).

"nursery rune /" was published in *Pool: a journal of poetry*, Issue #12 (2013).

"Jean Berko Gleason" originally appeared in *The Literary Review*, Summer 2013 (Vol. 56 Issue 02).

"A Reading" first appeared in *Conjunctions*, #60 (In Absentia), July 2013. It subsequently appeared in *Under the Sign* (Penguin 2013).

"What Dorothea Did" originally appeared in *Coconut* (#15).

"Philologist Disaster" first appeared in *fur(l) parachute* (BookThug 2013).

"New Romantics" originally appeared in *Black Warrior Review* No. 38.1, Fall/Winter 2011, and was published in *My Daughter La Chola* (Ahsahta Press, 2013).

The poem "Laneway" originally appeared in *The Capilano Review* issue 3.13 (2011). A modified version of "Laneway" appeared in *Tuft* (Book Thug 2013).

"Homosexual Interracial Dating in the South" was first published in *PANK*. Text found in *Home Taxidermy for Pleasure and Profit* by Albert B. Farnham.

"Sestina" originally appeared in *VOLT* (#18, 2013).

"Tower Sonnet" first appeared in *New American Writing* 31.

"Citizens United v. Federal Election Commission" was originally published in *Corporate Relations*, Burning Deck Press, 2014.

Apollinaire's "Inscription . . ." appeared in *The Poetry Project* newsletter #237 (December 2012 – January 2013 issue), published by the Poetry Project.

"Words 46,740 thru 47,047—That's to Say Page 159—of a Novel-in-Progress," originally appeared in *Colorado Review*, Fall 2013, 146.

"No More" was first published in *Poetry* in March 2013.

Excerpt from Citizen originally appeared in *Poetry* Magazine.

"Case" originally appeared in *Jacket2*.

Contributors

EMILY ABENDROTH is a writer and artist currently living in Philadelphia. Her print publications include]Exclosures[from Ahsahta Press and the chapbooks *NOTWITHSTANDING shoring*, *FLUMMOX* (Little Red Leaves), *Exclosures 1-8* (Albion Press), *Property : None* (a multimedia broadside project from Taproot Editions), *3 Exclosures* (Zumbar Press) and *Toward Eadward Forward* (horse less press). She was recently the recipient of a 2013 Pew Fellowship in Poetry. She is also an active member of the grassroots coalition Decarcerate PA and co-creator of the project *Address This!* which offers innovative radical/educational reading courses via correspondence to individuals incarcerated throughout Pennsylvania.

CA AIKEN is a writer and poet from Chicago, IL. "Hotspur: Esperance ma Comforte" is an excerpt from her unpublished manuscript, *Riots and Honors*, a prose-poem hybrid novel with roots in Shakespeare's Henriad.

TOBY ALTMAN is the author of two chapbooks, *Tender Industrial Fabric* (Greying Ghost, 2015) and *Asides* (Furniture Press, 2012). His poems can or will be found in *The Black Warrior Review, Diagram, The Laurel Review,* and other journals.

RAE ARMANTROUT's book *Versed* (Wesleyan) won the 2010 Pulitzer prize for poetry. Her book *Just Saying* was published by Wesleyan in 2013. A new book, *Itself,* is forthcoming from the same press in 2015. Armantrout lives and teaches in San Diego.

REBECCA BATES is a journalist and poet living in New York. Her poetry has appeared in the *Believer, Gulf Coast, No, Dear, Powder Keg, Lit,* and elsewhere. She is an assistant editor at *Condé Nast,* and her other writing can also be found in the *Guernica Daily, The New Inquiry, NYLON, NYLON Guys,* and elsewhere.

CHARLES BERNSTEIN is author of *Recalculating* (University of Chicago Press, 2013), *Attack of the Difficult Poems: Essays and Inventions* (Chicago, 2011), and *All the Whiskey in Heaven: Selected Poems* (Farrar, Straus and Giroux, 2010). He is Donald T. Regan Professor of English and Comparative Literature at the University of Pennsylvania, where he is co-director of PennSound <writing.upenn.edu/pennsound>. More info at epc.buffalo.edu.

MEI-MEI BERSSENBRUGGE was born in Beijing and grew up in Massachusetts. She is the author of 12 books of poetry, including *Empathy* (Station Hill), *Four Year Old Girl* (Kelsey Street), *I Love Artists: New and Selected Poems,* (University of California) and *Hello, the Roses* (New Directions), finalist for the *LA Times* Book Award. She has collaborated with many artists, including Kiki Smith and Richard Tuttle. She lives in northern New Mexico and New York City.

NATHAN BLAKE's chapbook *Going Home Nowhere and Fast* is available from Winged City Press. He is currently an MFA candidate at Virginia Tech.

AMARANTH BORSUK's most recent book is *As We Know* (Subito, 2014), a collaboration with Andy Fitch. She is the author of *Handiwork* (Slope Editions, 2012), and, with Brad Bouse, *Between Page and Screen* (Siglio Press, 2012). *Abra*, a collaboration with Kate Durbin forthcoming from 1913 Press, recently received an NEA-sponsored Expanded Artists' Books grant from the Center for Book and Paper Arts at Columbia College Chicago and will be issued in 2014 as an artist's book and iPad app created by Ian Hatcher. Amaranth teaches in the MFA in Creative Writing and Poetics at The University of Washington, Bothell.

JOHN BRADLEY is the author of *You Don't Know What You Don't Know* (CSU Poetry Center), *War on Words* (BlazeVox), and *Trancelumination* (Lowbrow Press). His most recent book is *One Day You a Mountain Shall Be: The Lost Poetry of Cheng Hui* (Finishing Line Press). He teaches at Northern Illinois University.

HANNAH BROOKS-MOTL currently lives in Chicago. She is the author of the chapbook *The Montaigne Result* (Song Cave, 2013) and the full-length collection *The New Years* (Rescue Press, 2014). "Twenty-Nine Sonnets of Eitenne de la Boétie" is from a manuscript that raids the first volume of Michel de Montaigne's *Essays*. The title and quoted language are from Donald Frame's translation.

ROBERT BRUNO is a writer and pop culture enthusiast. Bruno's recent work can also be found in *Yalobusha Review*.

C.S. CARRIER's books include */anode a/node an/ode* (Horse Less Press 2014), *Mantle* (H_ NGM_N Books 2013), and *After Dayton* (Four Way Books 2008). He currently lives in Clarksville, Arkansas.

KEN CHEN is the Executive Director of The Asian American Writers' Workshop, a national nonprofit dedicated to inventing the future of Asian American intellectual culture, and the 2009 recipient of the Yale Series of Younger Poets Award for his poetry collection *Juvenilia*. A founding contributor to Arts & Letters Daily, he is one of the founders of CultureStrike, a national pro-immigration movement which organized 300 writers to boycott Arizona in the wake of SB1070.

MAXINE CHERNOFF is the author of fourteen books of poetry and six of fiction. Her most recent poetry collections are *Here* (Counterpath, 2014), *Without* (Shearsman, 2012), *To Be Read in the Dark* (Omnidawn, 2011), and *The Turning* (Apogee, 2008). With Paul Hoover she received the 2009 PEN USA Translation Prize for *The Selected Works of Friedrich Hoelderlin* (Omnidawn 2008), and in 2013 she received an NEA Fellowship in Poetry. Two of her books of fiction were finalists for the Northern California Book Award (1996 and 2002), and her book of stories, *Signs of Devotion*, was a 2003 NYT Notable Book of the Year. She has been a Visiting International Scholar at the University of Exeter in England, taught in the Prague Summer Workshops, and for SLS in St Petersberg, Russia. In addition, she has read her poetry in Belgium, Scotland,

Brazil, and China. Chair of Creative Writing at SFSU, she edits the long-running poetry journal, *New American Writing*.

JOHN COLETTI is the author of *SKASERS*, a half-book with Anselm Berrigan (Flowers & Cream 2012), *Mum Halo* (Rust Buckle Books 2010), *Same Enemy Rainbow* (fewer & further 2008), and *Physical Kind* (Yo-Yo-Labs 2005). Other recent projects include a libretto for Excelsior, an opera composed by Caleb Burhans and commissioned by Chicago's Fifth House Ensemble (premiered in 2013) and a forthcoming book, *Deep Code*, will be published by City Lights Books in the fall of 2014.

CACONRAD's PACE The Nation Project is touring the U.S. to ask poets how to repair our war-obsessed nation. He is the author of seven books including *ECODEVIANCE: (Soma)tics for the Future Wilderness* (Wave Books, 2014), *A BEAUTIFUL MARSUPIAL AFTERNOON* (WAVE Books, 2012) and *The Book of Frank* (WAVE Books, 2010). A 2014 Lannan Fellow, a 2013 MacDowell Fellow, and a 2011 Pew Fellow, he also conducts workshops on (Soma)tic poetry and Ecopoetics. Visit him online at http://CAConrad.blogspot.com

KATHRYN COWLES's first book of poems, *Eleanor, Eleanor, not your real name*, won the 2008 Brunsman Poetry Prize. Recent poems and poem-photograph hybrids have appeared in *Diagram, The Offending Adam, Drunken Boat, Word for/ Word, Versal, Forklift: Ohio*, and the Academy of American Poets Poem-a-Day. She teaches at Hobart and William Smith Colleges in the Finger Lakes region of New York and is a poetry and hybrid-forms editor at *Seneca Review*.

MÓNICA DE LA TORRE is the author of four poetry collections—*Public Domain* (Roof Books) and *Talk Shows* (Switchback) and two collections in Spanish—and the chapbooks *Four* (Switchback) and *The Happy End* (Song Cave). Born and raised in Mexico City, she has translated numerous Latin American poets and coedited, with Michael Wiegers, the collection *Reversible Monuments: Contemporary Mexican Poetry* (Copper Canyon Press, 2002). She frequently collaborates with artists and writers, as with Collective Task. *Taller de Taquimecanografía*, published in Mexico City, is the result of another collaboration. Recently, her work has been published in *Aufgabe, Art in America, Convolution, frieze*, and Triple Canopy's *Corrected Slogans*. She is senior editor at *BOMB Magazine*.

BRETT DEFRIES was born in Topeka, KS. His work has appeared in *FENCE, Colorado Review, Konundrum Engine Literary Review*, and elsewhere. A chapbook was published by *New Delta Review* in 2012. He is currently a PhD candidate in English at the University of Iowa and lives in Iowa City with Emily Jones.

LATASHA N. NEVADA DIGGS is the author of *TwERK* (Belladonna* 2013). She has been published widely and her performance work has been featured at The Kitchen, Exit Art, Brooklyn Museum, The Whitney, MoMa, Queens Museum and The Walker Center. As a curator/director, she has staged events at El Museo del Barrio, Lincoln Center Out of Doors, Symphony Space, The David Rubenstein Atrium and BAM Café. A recipient of several awards, residencies and fellowships, LaTasha, along with Greg Tate, are the founders and editors of *Coon Bidness*, *yoYo/SO4* Magazine.

KATE DURBIN is a Los Angeles-based writer and artist. She is author of *The Ravenous Audience* (Akashic Books, 2009), *E! Entertainment* (Wonder), and co-author of *Abra*, forthcoming as an iPad app and artist book with the help of a grant from Center for Book and Paper Arts at Columbia College Chicago. She has also published five chapbooks. She is founding editor of *Gaga Stigmata*, and her tumblr project, *Women as Objects*, archives the teen girl tumblr aesthetic. Her projects have been anthologized and featured by *Poets and Writers*, *Salon.com*, *Huffington Post*, *The New Yorker*, *Spex*, NPR, *Hyperallergic,com*, *poets.org*, *Lana Turner: A Journal of Poetry and Opinion*, Yale's *The American Scholar*, *The Rumpus*, the *&NOW Innovative Writing Awards*, and others.

PETER EIRICH earned his two poetry degrees first from UCLA then NYU respectively. His work has been published in *Lana Turner* and *The Boston Review*'s Poet Sampler. He grew up first in Europe then the States. He lived in Los Angeles for a time and now permanently in Harlem, New York.

LISA FISHMAN is the author of *24 Pages and other poems*, forthcoming on Wave Books, 2015; *F L O W E R C A R T* (Ahsahta Press, 2011); *The Happiness Experiment* (Ahsahta, 2008), and three other full-length collections as well as several chapbooks. She lives in Orfordville, Wisconsin and teaches at Columbia College Chicago.

ANDY FITCH's most recent books are *Sixty Morning Talks* and (with Amaranth Borsuk) *As We Know*. Ugly Duckling soon will release his *Sixty Morning Walks* and *Sixty Morning Wlaks*. With Cristiana Baik, he is currently assembling the *Letter Machine Book of Interviews*. He has a collaborative book forthcoming from 1913 Press. He edits Essay Press and teaches in the University of Wyoming's MFA program.

OSSIAN FOLEY is a poet and man of the sea. *Of: Vol. I* was published in 2013 by Ugly Duckling Presse. With Jim Longley, Ossian edits *LVNG Magazine*. He lives with his dog, Satchel.

LOGAN FRY edits *Flag + Void* with Matthew Moore, contributes to *The Volta Blog*, and has writing featured in/forthcoming from *Boston Review*, *Bestoned*, *The Cultural Society*, *Denver Quarterly*, *Hardly Doughnuts*, and *Reality Hands*. An Ohio native, he lives in Austin, Texas, and simulacrates at bathosmtn.tumblr.com.

COLIN FULTON is Canadian. He has been alive for twenty-seven years, and lives and studies in the city of Montreal. *Life Experience Coolant* is his first book.

FORREST GANDER recently collaborated with Raúl Zurita on *Pinholes in the Night: Essential Poems from Latin America* and with the butoh dancers Eiko and Koma on the book of poems titled *Eiko & Koma*. Two other new titles have just been released in the U.S.: *Panic Cure: Poetry from Spain for the 21st Century* and *Fungus Skull Eye Wing: Poems by Alfonso D'Aquino*.

ANGELA GENUSA is a writer and artist. She is the author of *Composition* (Gauss PDF, 2014), *Twenty Six Wikipedia Articles* (PediaPress, 2103), *Musée du Service des Objets Trouvés* (PediaPress, 2013), *Spam Bibliography* (Troll Thread, 2013); *Tender Buttons and Jane Doe* (Gauss PDF, 2013); *Highlights for Ren* (Lulu, 2013), *onlinedating.teenadultdating/Adult-Dating* (Lulu, 2012) and *The Package Insert of Sorrows* (Lulu, 2011). Her book *Simone's Embassy* is forthcoming from Truck Books.

LARA GLENUM is the author of four books of poetry, including *The Hounds of No, Maximum Gaga*, and *Pop Corpse!*—all from Action Books—as well as *All Hopped Up On Fleshy Dumdums* (Spork Books). She is also the co-editor of *Gurlesque*, an anthology of contemporary women's poetry and visual art (Saturnalia Books). She is an associate professor in the MFA Program at Louisiana State University.

JUDITH GOLDMAN is the author of *Vocoder, DeathStar/Rico-chet*, and *l.b.; or, catenaries*; a new book, *___Mt. (blank mount)*, is in the works. From 2005-2009, she co-edited the yearly journal *War and Peace* with Leslie Scalapino, while she currently edits poetry features for the online academic journal *Postmodern Culture*. She has taught creative writing and media aesthetics at University of Chicago and was the Holloway Poet at UC Berkeley in 2011. She joined the core faculty of the Poetics Program at University at Buffalo in 2012.

DAVID GORIN's writing has appeared in *A Public Space, Best New Poets 2011, The Believer, Boston Review, The Claudius App*, and elsewhere. He holds an MFA from the Iowa Writers' Workshop and is completing a PhD in English Literature at Yale. He is a poetry blogger for the *Boston Review* and runs the *WAVEMACHINE* poetry series in New Haven, Connecticut.

KATE GREENSTREET's book *Young Tambling* was published by Ahsahta Press in 2013. Her previous books are *The Last 4 Things* and *case sensitive*, also with Ahsahta. For more information, see kickingwind.com.

BRENDA HILLMAN has published chapbooks with Penumbra Press, a+bend press, and EmPress; she is the author of nine full-length collections from Wesleyan University Press, the most recent of which are *Practical Water* (2009) and *Seasonal Works with Letters on Fire* (2013). With Patricia Dienstfrey, she edited *The Grand Permission: New Writings on Poetics and Motherhood* (Wesleyan, 2003). Hillman teaches at St. Mary's College of California where she is the Olivia C. Filippi Professor of Poetry; she is an activist for social and environmental justice and lives in the San Francisco Bay Area.

KEVIN HOLDEN's book *Solar* won the 2014 Fence Modern Poets Prize. He is the author of two chapbooks, *Identity* (Cannibal Books) and *Alpine* (White Queen Press). His poetry has appeared in such places as *Conjunctions*, *jubilat*, *The New Yorker*, *1913*, *Harp & Altar*, and *Colorado Review*, and was included in the recent anthology *The Arcadia Project* (Ahsahta Press). He also translates poetry, and that work has been published in *Aufgabe*, *Double Change*, *Inventory* and other journals. He is currently working toward a PhD in comparative literature at Yale.

HARMONY HOLIDAY received her MFA in Poetry from Columbia University, where she completed the manuscript for her first book *Negro League Baseball*, which was published by Fence Books in 2011 and received the press's Motherwell Prize. Her follow-up to the that, *Go Find your Father/A Famous Blues*, a "dos-a-dos" book featuring poetry, letters, and essays, is due out on USC's budding imprint Ricochet Editions, in January 2014.

JANIS BUTLER HOLM lives in Athens, Ohio, where she has served as Associate Editor for *Wide Angle*, the film journal. Her prose, poems, and performance pieces have appeared in small-press, national, and international magazines. Her plays have been produced in the U.S., Canada, and England.

DARREL ALEJANDRO HOLNES is from Panama City and the former Canal Zone of Panamá. He studied art at the Universidad del Arte Ganexa, music at the Instituto Nacional de Música, and creative writing at the Universities of Houston and Michigan, the latter from which he earned a Masters of Fine Arts degree. His poetry has been published in the *Best American Experimental Writing* anthology, *Callaloo*, *The Caribbean Writer*, *The Potomac*, *MEADE*, *Lambda Literary*, *Assaracus*, *Weave Magazine*, *The Feminist Wire*, *The Paris American*, *Kweli*, featured on the *Best American Poetry* blog, and elsewhere in print and online. He is the co-author of *PRIME: Poetry & Conversations* (Sibling Rivalry Press, 2014). His plays have been recognized by the Kennedy Center, and read and produced in regional and university theaters throughout the US. He was a "waiter" at the Bread Loaf Writers Conference, and is a Cave Canem, CantoMundo, and VCFA fellow. He currently teaches at Rutgers University and New York University, consults the United Nations, and writes and resides in New York, NY. www.darrelholnes.com

KATHLEEN JANESCHEK is a writer from a small town in Southwest Michigan. Currently, she is a student at the University of Michigan studying mathematics and creative writing. Formerly, she was employed in a library as a page. She has published poetry in *Inner Landscapes: Writers Respond to the Art of Virginia Dehn*, but for the time is focusing on writing short stories.

LISA JARNOT is the author of six books of poetry and *Robert Duncan: The Ambassador From Venus, A Comprehensive Biography*. She lives in Jackson Heights, Queens, and works as a freelance gardener.

ANDREW JORON is the author of *Trance Archive: New and Selected Poems* (City Lights, 2010). Joron's previous poetry collections include *The Removes* (Hard Press, 1999), *Fathom* (Black Square Editions, 2003), and *The Sound Mirror* (Flood Editions, 2008). *The Cry at Zero*, a selection of his prose poems and critical essays, was published by Counterpath Press in 2007. From the German, he has translated the *Literary Essays* of Marxist-Utopian philosopher Ernst Bloch (Stanford University Press, 1998) and *The Perpetual Motion Machine* by the proto-Dada fantasist Paul Scheerbart (Wakefield Press, 2011). Joron teaches creative writing at San Francisco State University.

Poet/performer/librettist DOUGLAS KEARNEY's third poetry collection, *Patter* (Red Hen Press, 2014) examines miscarriage, infertility, and parenthood. His second, *The Black Automaton* (Fence Books, 2009), was a National Poetry Series selection. He has received residencies/fellowships from Cave Canem, The Rauschenberg Foundation, and others. His work has appeared in a number of journals, including *Poetry*, *nocturnes*, *Pleiades*, and *Callaloo*. Raised in Altadena, CA, he lives with his family in California's Santa Clarita Valley. He teaches at CalArts.

DANIEL KHALASTCHI is the author of two books of poetry, *Manoleria* (Tupelo Press, 2011) and *Tradition* (McSweeney's, 2015). A former fellow at the Fine Arts Work Center in Provincetown, his poems have appeared in a variety of journals, including *Colorado Review*, *Columbia Poetry Review*, *Court Green*, *Denver Quarterly*, *Iowa Review*, *jubilat*, *Ninth Letter*, *Thermos*, and *1913: A Journal of Forms*. Daniel currently lives in Iowa City where he is the associate director of the University of Iowa's Frank N. Magid Center for Undergraduate Writing. He is also the co-founder and managing editor of Rescue Press.

PAULA KONEAZNY grew up in Chippewa Falls, WI and graduated from UW-Madison with a degree in Political Science and French in 1970. She received a Masters in English from Sonoma State in 1998. Her poetry often incorporates French and reflects her interest in art, photography, language, the natural sciences, cosmology and history. Her approach to writing is investigative. She holds a high regard for wit and uncomfortable historical facts, as well as exactitude and weirdness in poetry. Her chapbook *Installation* (2012) is available from Tarpaulin Sky Press. She is currently an Assistant Editor of *VOLT*.

JENNIFER KRONOVET is the author of the poetry collection *Awayward*. She co-translated *The Acrobat*, the selected poems of experimental Yiddish poet Celia Dropkin. Her poems have appeared in *American Poetry Review*, *Bomb*, *Boston Review*, *Fence*, *The Nation*, *A Public Space*, and elsewhere. She has taught at Beijing Normal University, Columbia University, and Washington University in St. Louis, and she currently lives in Guangzhou, China.

ANN LAUTERBACH, poet and essayist, is the author of nine books of poetry, a collection of essays, and numerous works on and with visual artists. She is co-Chair of Writing in the Milton Avery Graduate School of the Arts and Schwab Professor of Languages and Literature at Bard College. She lives in Germantown, New York.

PAUL LEGAULT is the author of four books of poetry: *The Madeleine Poems* (Omnidawn 2010), *The Other Poems* (Fence, 2011), *The Emily Dickinson Reader* (McSweeney's, 2012), and *The New York Poems* (Fence, 2015). Currently, he is a Writer in Residence at Washington University in St. Louis, and can be found here: www.theotherpaul.com.

SHANNON MAGUIRE holds an MFA in Creative Writing (Poetry) from the University of Guelph. Her first collection, *fur(l) parachute*, was a finalist for the Robert Kroetsch Award for Innovative Poetry and the Golden Crown Award for Lesbian Poetry. Her second collection, *Myrmurs*, is forthcoming from BookThug in 2015. Shannon is a doctoral student in English and Film Studies at Wilfrid Laurier University where she studies queer and Métis poetics and is a Teaching Assistant in English and Women and Gender Studies.

FARID MATUK is the author of *This Isa Nice Neighborhood* (Letter Machine Editions) and *My Daughter La Chola* (Ahsahta). His poems have appeared in *6x6*, *The Baffler*, *Boston Review*, *Denver Quarterly*, *The Iowa Review*, and *Poetry*, among others. Matuk is a contributor to *Scubadivers and Chrysanthemums: Essays On the Poetry of Araki Yasusada* (Shearsman) and to the poetry anthologies *American Odyssesy* (Dalkey Archive) and *Poets Of the Americlypse* (Counterpath), among others. He serves as poetry editor for *Fence* and as contributing editor at *The Volta*. Matuk lives in Tucson with the poet Susan Briante and teaches in the MFA program at the University of Arizona.

KIM MINKUS is a poet with three books of poetry *9 Freight* (LINEbooks 2007), *Thresh* (Snare Books 2009) and *Tuft* (BookThug 2013). She has had reviews, poetry and fiction published in *The Capilano Review*, *FRONT Magazine*, *West Coast Line*, *The Poetic Front*, and *Jacket*. Most recently, she co-edited an issue of *The Capilano Review* that focused on innovative narrative. She is a Creative Writing instructor at Capilano University in North Vancouver, British Columbia.

RAJIV MOHABIR's first full-length collection of poems *The Taxidermist's Cut*, winner of the 2014 Intro Prize in Poetry, is forthcoming from Four Way Books. A VONA, Kundiman, and American Institute of Indian Studies language fellow, some of his poetry and translations appear in journals such as *The Prairie Schooner*, *Crab Orchard Review*, *Drunken Boat*, *Anti-*, *Great River Review*, *PANK*, and *Aufgabe*. Having completed his MFA in poetry and translation from Queens College, CUNY, he is currently pursuing a PhD from the University of Hawai'i, at Manoa.

NICOLAS MUGAVERO lives and works in Raleigh, North Carolina. He co-curates orworse. net and orworsepress.net with Chris Sylvester and Shiv Kotecha. He has published books with Troll Thread Press and Gauss PDF. His poetic practice can best be described as one of diminishing returns.

LAURA MULLEN is the author of *Enduring Freedom: A Little Book of Mechanical Brides*, *The Surface*, *After I Was Dead*, *Subject*, *Dark Archive*, *The Tales of Horror*, and *Murmur*.

Recognitions for her poetry include Ironwood's Stanford Prize, a National Endowment for the Arts Fellowship and a Rona Jaffe Award. She has had several MacDowell Fellowships and is a frequent visitor to the Jack Kerouac School of Disembodied Poetics at Naropa. Her work has been widely anthologized and is included in *Postmodern American Poetry*, and *American Hybrid* (Norton), as well as *I'll Drown My Book: Conceptual Writing by Women* (Les Figues). Undersong, the composer Jason Eckardt's setting of "The Distance (This)" (from *Subject*) was released on Mode records. Mullen is the McElveen Professor in English at LSU and a contributing editor for the on-line poetry site *The Volta*. Her eighth collection—*Complicated Grief*—is forthcoming from Solid Objects in Fall of 2014.

Born in the Mekong Delta and raised in the Washington, D.C. area, HOA NGUYEN studied Poetics at New College of California in San Francisco. With the poet Dale Smith, Nguyen founded *Skanky Possum*, a poetry journal and book imprint in Austin, TX, their home of 14 years. She is the author of eight books and chapbooks including *As Long As Trees Last* (Wave, 2012). She currently lives in Toronto where she teaches poetics in a private workshop and at Ryerson University. Wave Books will release *Red Juice*, a gathering of her early, uncollected poems, in September 2014.

JENA OSMAN's books of poems include *Corporate Relations* (Burning Deck Press, 2014), *Public Figures* (Wesleyan University Press, 2012), *The Network* (Fence Books 2010, selected for the 2009 National Poetry Series), *An Essay in Asterisks* (Roof Books, 2004) and *The Character* (Beacon Press, winner of the 1998 Barnard New Women Poets Prize). The piece selected for this anthology was also set to music by the composer Ted Hearne in his "Sound from the Bench." Osman was a 2006 Pew Fellow in the Arts, and has received grants for her poetry from the National Endowment for the Arts, the New York Foundation for the Arts, The Pennsylvania Council on the Arts, the Howard Foundation, and the Fund for Poetry. She teaches in the MFA Creative Writing Program at Temple University.

New York Review Books will publish RON PADGETT's *Zone: Selected Poems of Guillaume Apollinaire* in 2015. Padgett's *How Long* was a 2012 Pulitzer Prize Finalist in Poetry. His *Collected Poems* (Coffee House Press) received the 2014 *L.A. Times* Best Book of Poetry prize and the William Carlos Williams Award from the Poetry Society of America.

ED PAVLIĆ's next books will be *Let's Let That Are Not Yet : Inferno* (2015) and *'Who Can Afford to Improvise?': Black Music and James Baldwin's Political Aesthetic* (2015). His most recent books are *Visiting Hours at the Color Line* (2013), *But Here Are Small Clear Refractions* (2009) and *Winners Have Yet to be Announced: A Song for Donny Hathaway* (2008). Others include *Paraph of Bone & Other Kinds of Blue* (2001), *Crossroads Modernism* (2002), and *Labors Lost Left Unfinished* (2006).

M. NOURBESE PHILIP is an unembedded poet, essayist, novelist and playwright who lives in the space-time of the City of Toronto. She practised law in the City of Toronto for seven years before becoming a poet and writer. She has published four books of poetry including the seminal *She Tries Her Tongue; Her Silence Softly Breaks*, one novel and three collections of essays. Her most recent work is the conceptually innovative, book-length poem *Zong!*, which explodes the legal archive as it relates to slavery. Among her awards are numerous Canada Council and Ontario Arts Council grants, as well as the Pushcart Prize (USA, 1981), the Casa de las Americas Prize (Cuba, 1988), the Lawrence Foundation Prize (USA, 1994), and the Arts Foundation of Toronto Writing and Publishing Award (Toronto,1995), Dora Award finalist (1999). Her fellowships include Guggenheim (1990), McDowell (1991), and Rockefeller (Bellagio) (2005). She has been Writer-in-Residence at several universities.

VANESSA PLACE is CEO of VanessaPlace Inc., the world's first poetry corporation.

ARTUR (ARTŪRS) PUNTE was born in Riga in 1977. A graduate of the Gorky Institute of Literature in Moscow, he is a poet and media-artist and one of the founding members of Orbita* group. He is the author of three collections of poetry, most recently Стихотворные посвящения Артура Пунте (Artur Punte's Poetic Dedications, 2013). Punte has translated poetry from Latvian and at times writes in Latvian himself. He has co-edited the majority of books published by Orbita, including Антология современной русской поэзии Латвии (Anthology of Contemporary Russian Poetry of Latvia, 2008).
* Orbita is a creative collective of Russian poets and artists whose projects are dedicated to dialogue between genres and cultures. The collective was founded in Riga, Latvia in 1999. Since that time Orbita has published a series of almanacs of literature and visual art and a number of bilingual Russian-Latvian books of poetry, essays, art and photography. Additionally, Orbita has organized three "Word in Motion" festivals of poetic video and multi-media art in Latvia (in 2001, 2003 and 2007); issued three audio compact discs and a collection of poetic video clips; and created a number of multi-media poetry installations for galleries and museums. Orbita's projects have been recognized with many awards: The Latvian Writer's Union Annual Literature Award (2005); the Poetry Days Award (2007); the MAP Book Design Award (2009), and others.

CLAUDIA RANKINE is the author most recently of *Citizen: An American Lyric* and co-author of the *Racial Imaginary*.

ED ROBERSON is the author of six books of poetry, most recently *To See the Earth Before the End of the World*. He has been awarded the Shelly Memorial Award from the Poetry Society of America and the Iowa Poetry Prize and the *LA Times* Book Award, among others. A visiting writer/artist in residence at Northwestern University since 2007, he has also taught at the University of Chicago, the University of Pittsburg, and Rutgers University.

ELIZABETH ROBINSON is the author of several poetry collections, most recently, *Counterpart* and *Blue Heron*. Her mixed genre book *On Ghosts* was a 2013 finalist for the *Los Angeles Times* Book Award. Robinson has been a winner of the Fence Modern Poets Prize, the National Poetry Series, and the Foundation for Contemporary Arts Grants to Artists Award. She is a co-editor of Instance Press and the literary periodical *pallaksch.pallaksch*.

RYAN PAUL SCHAEFER received his M.F.A. in poetry from Brooklyn College and a B.A. in English from U.C. Berkeley; while at Berkeley he worked as an editor for the *Berkeley Poetry Review* and the *Cal Literary Arts Magazine* (CLAM); he was also the poetry editor at the *Brooklyn Review* in 2013. In 2014 he was a recipient of the Himan Brown Award. His work has appeared in *Five Quarterly (5Q)* and the *Berkeley Poetry Review*. He lives in the Bath Beach neighborhood of Brooklyn.

DANNIEL SCHOONEBEEK's first book of poems, *American Barricade*, was published by YesYes Books in 2014. A chapbook, *Family Album*, was published by Poor Claudia in 2013, and an EP of recorded poems, *Trench Mouth*, is also available from Black Cake Records. His work has appeared in *Poetry, Tin House, Boston Review, Fence, BOMB, jubilat, Indiana Review, Denver Quarterly*, and elsewhere. He writes a column on poetry for *The American Reader*, hosts the Hatchet Job reading series, and edits the PEN Poetry Series. In 2015, Poor Claudia will release his second book, a travelogue called *C'est la guerre*.

CHRISTOPHER STACKHOUSE is author of the chapbook *Slip* (Corollary Press); co-author of the image/text collaboration, *Seismosis* (1913 Press), which features Stackhouse's drawings in discourse with writer/translator John Keene's texts; and a volume of poems, *Plural* (Counterpath Press). Stackhouse's recent essays have been published in artist Kara Walker's monograph *Dust Jackets for The Niggerati* (Gregory R. Miller & Co.); online in the contemporary art magazine *Painter's Table*, an essay on painter Leland Bell; and in the forthcoming monograph *Basquiat: The Unknown Notebooks* (Skira Rizzoli) for the exhibition opening at The Brooklyn Museum April 2015. At the Maryland Institute College of Art he is Senior Thesis Faculty and a Visiting Critic at the Leroy E. Hoffberger School of Painting.

CHRIS SYLVESTER makes sisteract.tumblr.com, co-edits trollthread.tumblr.com (with Holly Melgard and Joey Yearous-Algozin) and orworse.net (with Nick Mugavero). His Instagram name is 'spreadsheet'. + Follow = Follow Back

JENNIFER TAMAYO is a performer, writer, and activist. She is the author of three collections of art and writing, most recently *YOU DA ONE* (Coconut Books, 2014). JT lives in Brooklyn and serves as the Managing Editor of Futurepoem.

ANNE WALDMAN is the author of over 40 collections of poetry, including the three-volume long poem *Iovis*. Co-founder with Allen Ginsberg of the Jack Kerouac School of Disembodied Poetics at Naropa University, she is internationally active in making poetry politically effective. The poet-in-residence for Bob Dylan's Rolling Thunder Revue, she has also twice won the International Poetry Championship Bout and was awarded the Shelly Memorial Award from the Poetry Society of America.

G.C. WALDREP's most recent books are *The Arcadia Project: North American Postmodern Pastoral* (Ahsahta, 2012), co-edited with Joshua Corey, and a chapbook, *Susquehanna* (Omnidawn, 2013). BOA Editions will release a long poem, *Testament*, in 2015. Waldrep lives in Lewisburg, Pa., where he teaches at Bucknell University, edits the journal *West Branch*, and serves as Editor-at-Large for *The Kenyon Review*.

MARJORIE WELISH's most recent book of poems is *In the Futurity Lounge / Asylum for Indeterminacy* (Coffee House Press, 2012). *Oaths? Questions?* (Granary Books, 2009), was demonstrated at Spaces of the Book, a conference on innovative artists' books, Trinity College, Cambridge, September 2013. *Of the Diagram: The work of Marjorie Welish* (Slought Foundation, 2003) compiles papers given at a conference devoted to her writing and art on April 5, 2002 at the University of Pennsylvania. A second conference occurred under the auspices of Poets and Critics at ParisEst, April 11-12, 2013. Marjorie Welish is a Guggenheim Foundation Fellow for 2014.

THE BECOMING is the first book of the WEST OF KINGDOM COME tetralogy, published by Calamari Press.

LYNN XU is the author of *Debts & Lessons* and *June*, a chapbook. She co-edits Canarium Books and lives in Marfa, Texas with her husband, the poet Joshua Edwards.

MATVEI YANKELEVICH is the author of the poetry collection *Alpha Donut* (United Artists Books) and the novella-in-fragments *Boris by the Sea* (Octopus Books), and the translator of *Today I Wrote Nothing: The Selected Writings of Daniil Kharms* (Overlook/Ardis). He is one of the founding editors of Ugly Duckling Presse, where he curates the Eastern European Poets Series.

JOEY YEAROUS-ALGOZIN is the author of *Holly Melgard's Friends and Family* (2014), *The Lazarus Project* (2011-2013) and *Zero Dark 30PT. Font*, among others. He is a member of TROLL THREAD and lives in Buffalo, NY.